Disney DuckTales

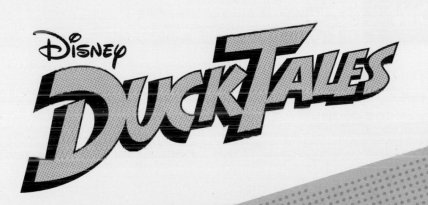

Facebook: **facebook.com/idwpublishing**
Twitter: **@idwpublishing**
YouTube: **youtube.com/idwpublishing**
Tumblr: **tumblr.idwpublishing.com**
Instagram: **instagram.com/idwpublishing**

ISBN: 978-1-68405-208-0   21 20 19 18   2 3 4 5

COVER ARTIST
MARCO GHIGLIONE

COVER COLORIST
LUCIO DE GIUSEPPE

LETTERER
TOM B. LONG

SERIES EDITORS
SARAH GAYDOS
and JOE HUGHES

COLLECTION EDITORS
JUSTIN EISINGER
and ALONZO SIMON

COLLECTION DESIGNER
CLYDE GRAPA

PUBLISHER
GREG GOLDSTEIN

Originally published as DUCKTALES issues #0–2.

Greg Goldstein, President & Publisher

Robbie Robbins, EVP & Sr. Art Director

Chris Ryall, Chief Creative Officer & Editor-in-Chief

Matthew Ruzicka, CPA, Chief Financial Officer

David Hedgecock, Associate Publisher

Laurie Windrow, Senior Vice President of Sales & Marketing

Lorelei Bunjes, VP of Digital Services

Eric Moss, Sr. Director, Licensing & Business Development

Ted Adams, Founder & CEO of IDW Media Holdings

Special Thanks to Carlotta Quattrocolo, Julie Dorris, Eugene Paraszczuk,
Chris Troise, Daniel Saeva, Manny Mederos, Roberto Santillo, Marco Ghiglione,
Stefano Attardi, Stefano Ambrosio, and Jonathan Manning.

BIG TROUBLE AT LITTLE LAKE
WRITER: JOE CARAMAGNA
LAYOUTS: PAOLO CAMPINOTI
PENCILS: ANDREA GREPPI
INKS: ROBERTA ZANOTTA
COLORIST: DARIO CALABRIA

THE REPEATING REVENGE OF THE SCREAMING DUCK
WRITER: JOE CARAMAGNA
ARTIST: GIANFRANCO FLORIO
COLORISTS: DARIO CALABRIA AND GIUSEPPE FONTANA

THE CHILLING SECRET OF THE LIGHTHOUSE
WRITER: JOE CARAMAGNA
ARTIST: LUCA USAI
COLORIST: GIUSEPPE FONTANA

THE GREAT EXPERIMENT OF THE WASHING MACHINE
WRITER: JOE CARAMAGNA
ARTIST: GIANFRANCO FLORIO
COLORISTS: GIUSEPPE FONTANA AND DARIO CALABRIA

OLD MONTEPLUMAGE HAD A CHICKEN
WRITER: JOEY CAVALIERI
ARTIST: GIANFRANCO FLORIO
COLORISTS: GIUSEPPE FONTANA AND DARIO CALABRIA

A VIKING AT MY DOOR!
WRITER: JOEY CAVALIERI
LAYOUT: ANTONELLO DALENA
CLEANUP: ANDREA GREPPI
INKS: ROBERTA ZANOTTA
COLORIST: GIUSEPPE FONTANA

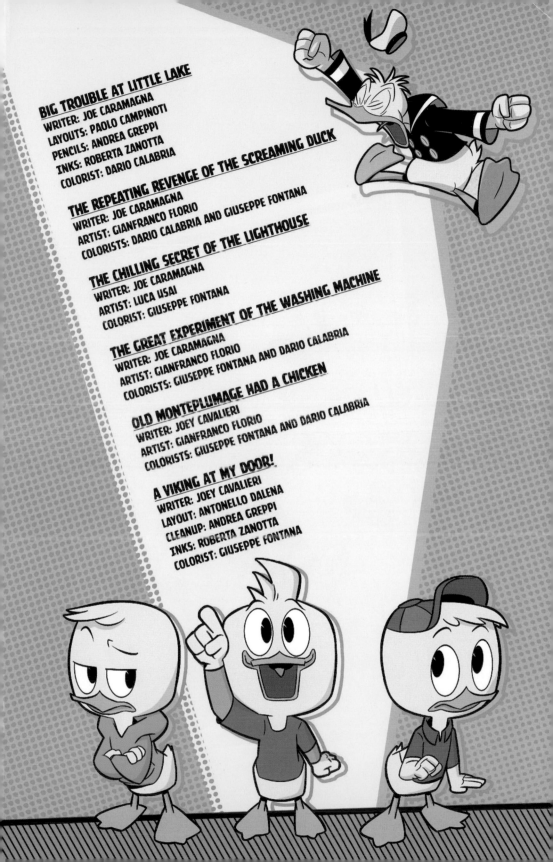

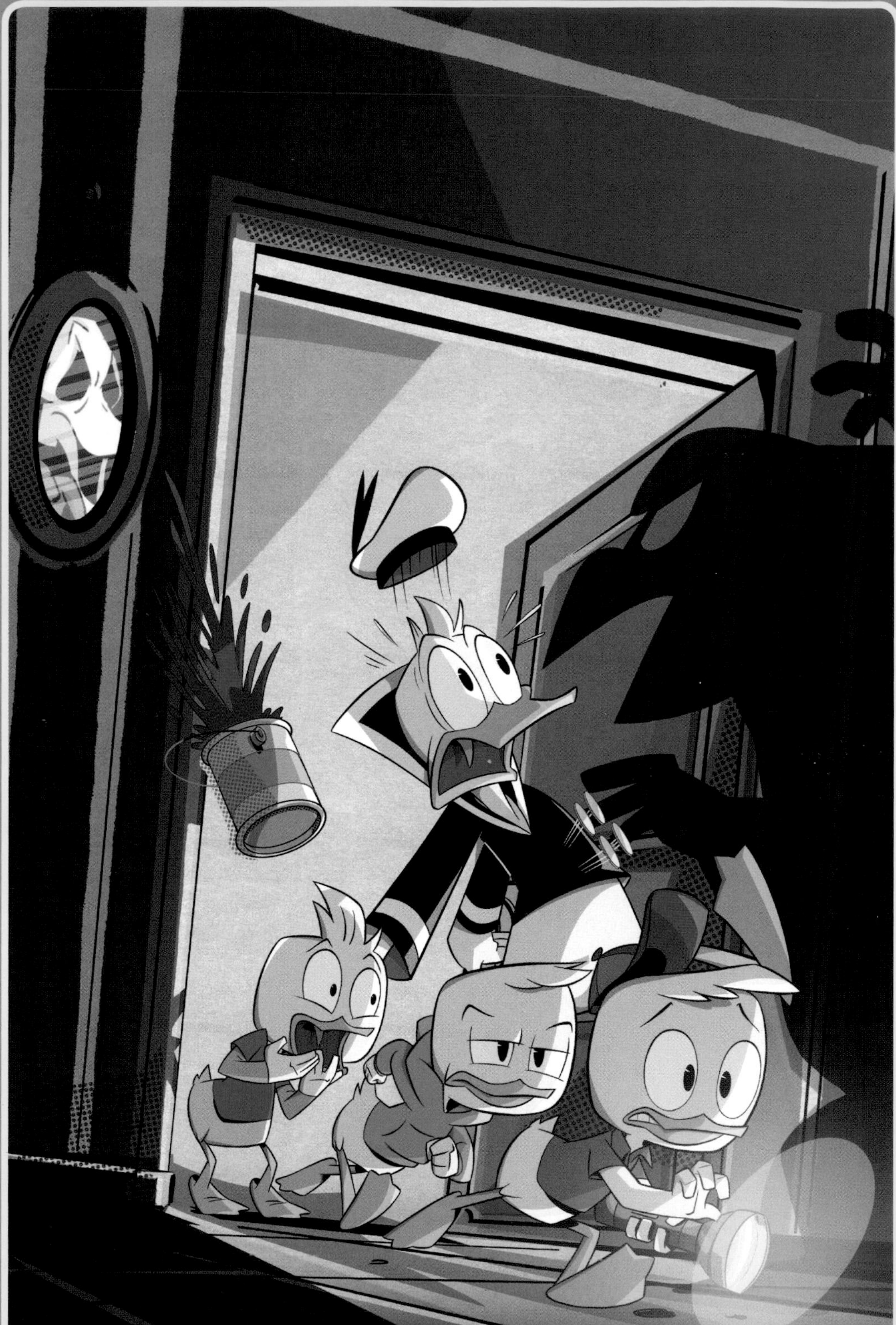

Art by Marco Ghiglione, Colors by Lucio De Guiseppe

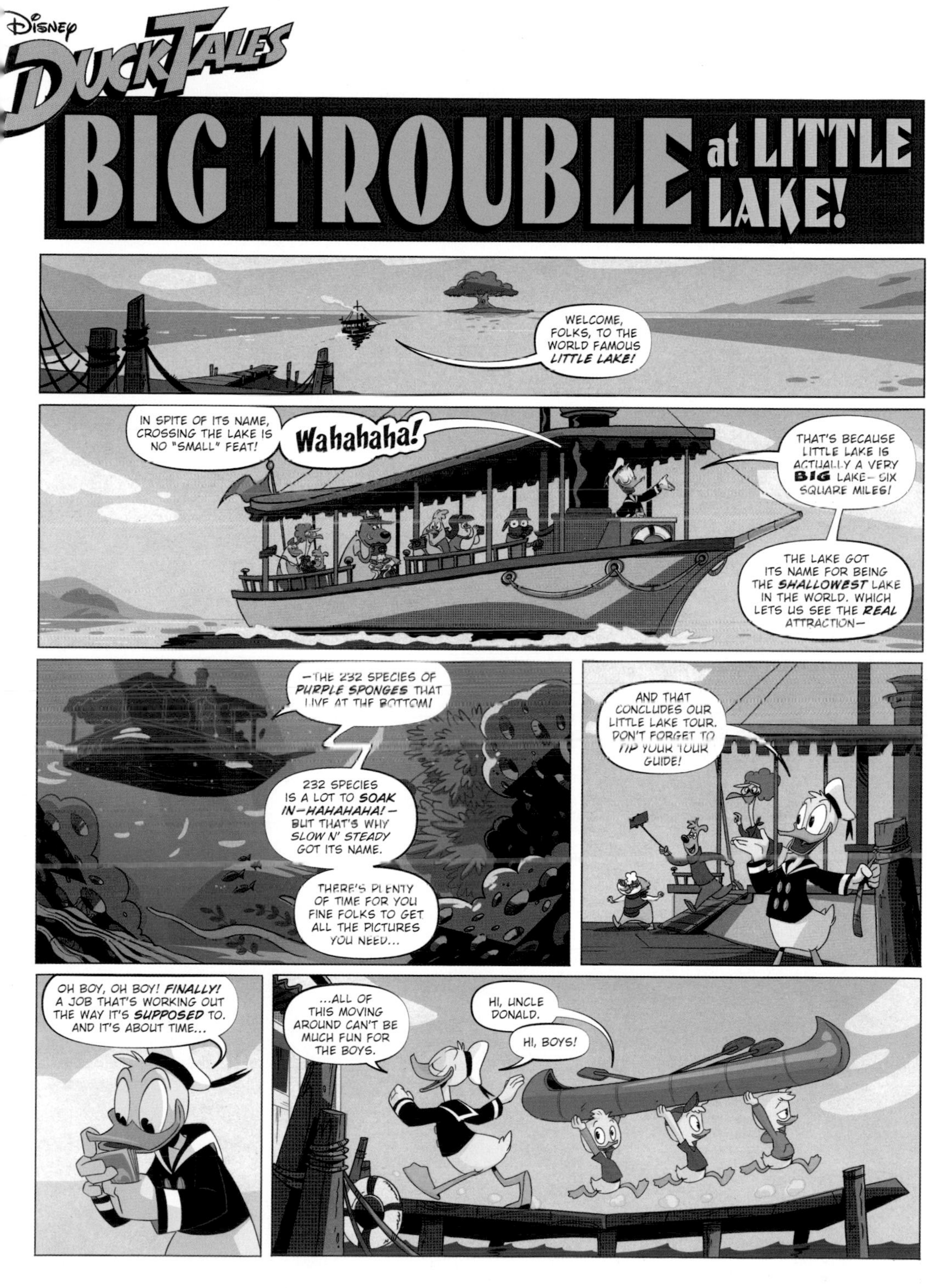
Disney
DuckTales
BIG TROUBLE at LITTLE LAKE!
WELCOME, FOLKS, TO THE WORLD FAMOUS LITTLE LAKE!
IN SPITE OF ITS NAME, CROSSING THE LAKE IS NO "SMALL" FEAT!
Wahahaha!
THAT'S BECAUSE LITTLE LAKE IS ACTUALLY A VERY BIG LAKE—SIX SQUARE MILES!
THE LAKE GOT ITS NAME FOR BEING THE SHALLOWEST LAKE IN THE WORLD. WHICH LETS US SEE THE REAL ATTRACTION—
—THE 232 SPECIES OF PURPLE SPONGES THAT LIVE AT THE BOTTOM!
232 SPECIES IS A LOT TO SOAK IN—HAHAHAHA!—BUT THAT'S WHY SLOW N' STEADY GOT ITS NAME.
THERE'S PLENTY OF TIME FOR YOU FINE FOLKS TO GET ALL THE PICTURES YOU NEED...
AND THAT CONCLUDES OUR LITTLE LAKE TOUR. DON'T FORGET TO TIP YOUR TOUR GUIDE!
OH BOY, OH BOY! FINALLY! A JOB THAT'S WORKING OUT THE WAY IT'S SUPPOSED TO. AND IT'S ABOUT TIME...
...ALL OF THIS MOVING AROUND CAN'T BE MUCH FUN FOR THE BOYS.
HI, UNCLE DONALD.
HI, BOYS!

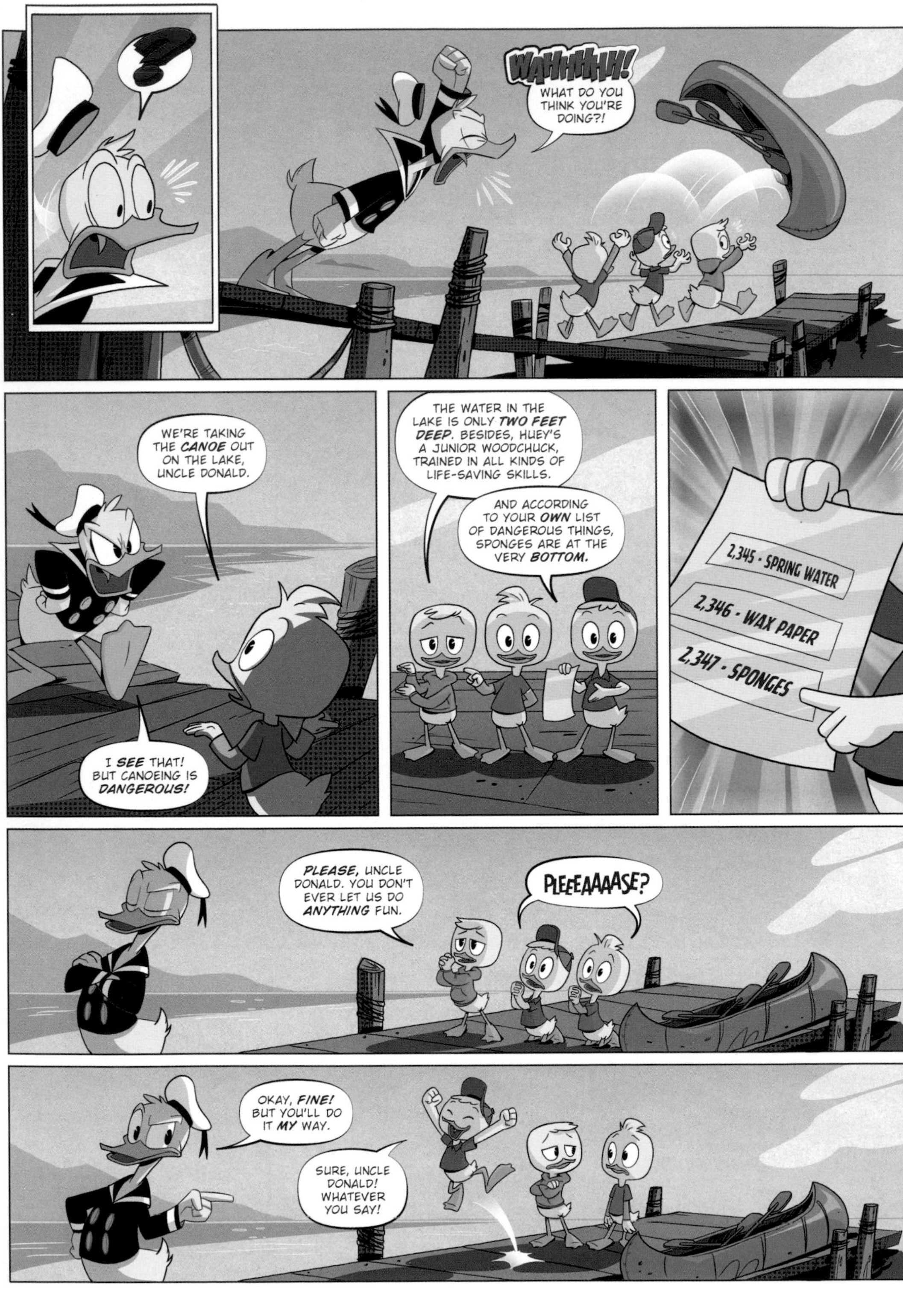

WAHHHHH!
WHAT DO YOU THINK YOU'RE DOING?!
WE'RE TAKING THE CANOE OUT ON THE LAKE, UNCLE DONALD.
I SEE THAT! BUT CANOEING IS DANGEROUS!
THE WATER IN THE LAKE IS ONLY TWO FEET DEEP. BESIDES, HUEY'S A JUNIOR WOODCHUCK, TRAINED IN ALL KINDS OF LIFE-SAVING SKILLS.
AND ACCORDING TO YOUR OWN LIST OF DANGEROUS THINGS, SPONGES ARE AT THE VERY BOTTOM.
2,345 - SPRING WATER
2,346 - WAX PAPER
2,347 - SPONGES
PLEASE, UNCLE DONALD. YOU DON'T EVER LET US DO ANYTHING FUN.
PLEEEAAAASE?
OKAY, FINE! BUT YOU'LL DO IT MY WAY.
SURE, UNCLE DONALD! WHATEVER YOU SAY!

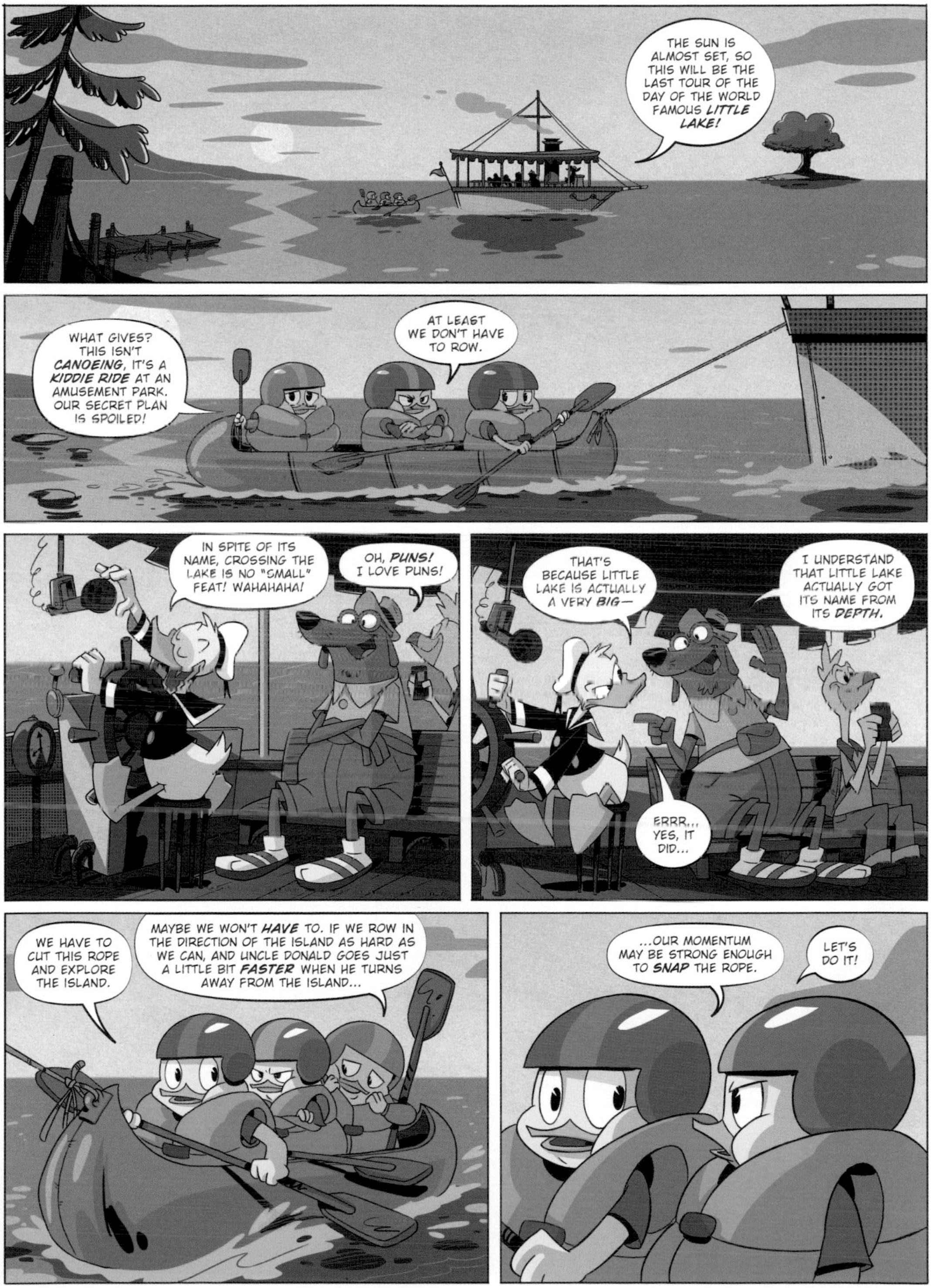

THE SUN IS ALMOST SET, SO THIS WILL BE THE LAST TOUR OF THE DAY OF THE WORLD FAMOUS LITTLE LAKE!
WHAT GIVES? THIS ISN'T CANOEING, IT'S A KIDDIE RIDE AT AN AMUSEMENT PARK. OUR SECRET PLAN IS SPOILED!
AT LEAST WE DON'T HAVE TO ROW.
IN SPITE OF ITS NAME, CROSSING THE LAKE IS NO "SMALL" FEAT! WAHAHAHA!
OH, PUNS! I LOVE PUNS!
THAT'S BECAUSE LITTLE LAKE IS ACTUALLY A VERY BIG—
I UNDERSTAND THAT LITTLE LAKE ACTUALLY GOT ITS NAME FROM ITS DEPTH.
ERRR... YES, IT DID...
WE HAVE TO CUT THIS ROPE AND EXPLORE THE ISLAND.
MAYBE WE WON'T HAVE TO. IF WE ROW IN THE DIRECTION OF THE ISLAND AS HARD AS WE CAN, AND UNCLE DONALD GOES JUST A LITTLE BIT FASTER WHEN HE TURNS AWAY FROM THE ISLAND...
...OUR MOMENTUM MAY BE STRONG ENOUGH TO SNAP THE ROPE.
LET'S DO IT!

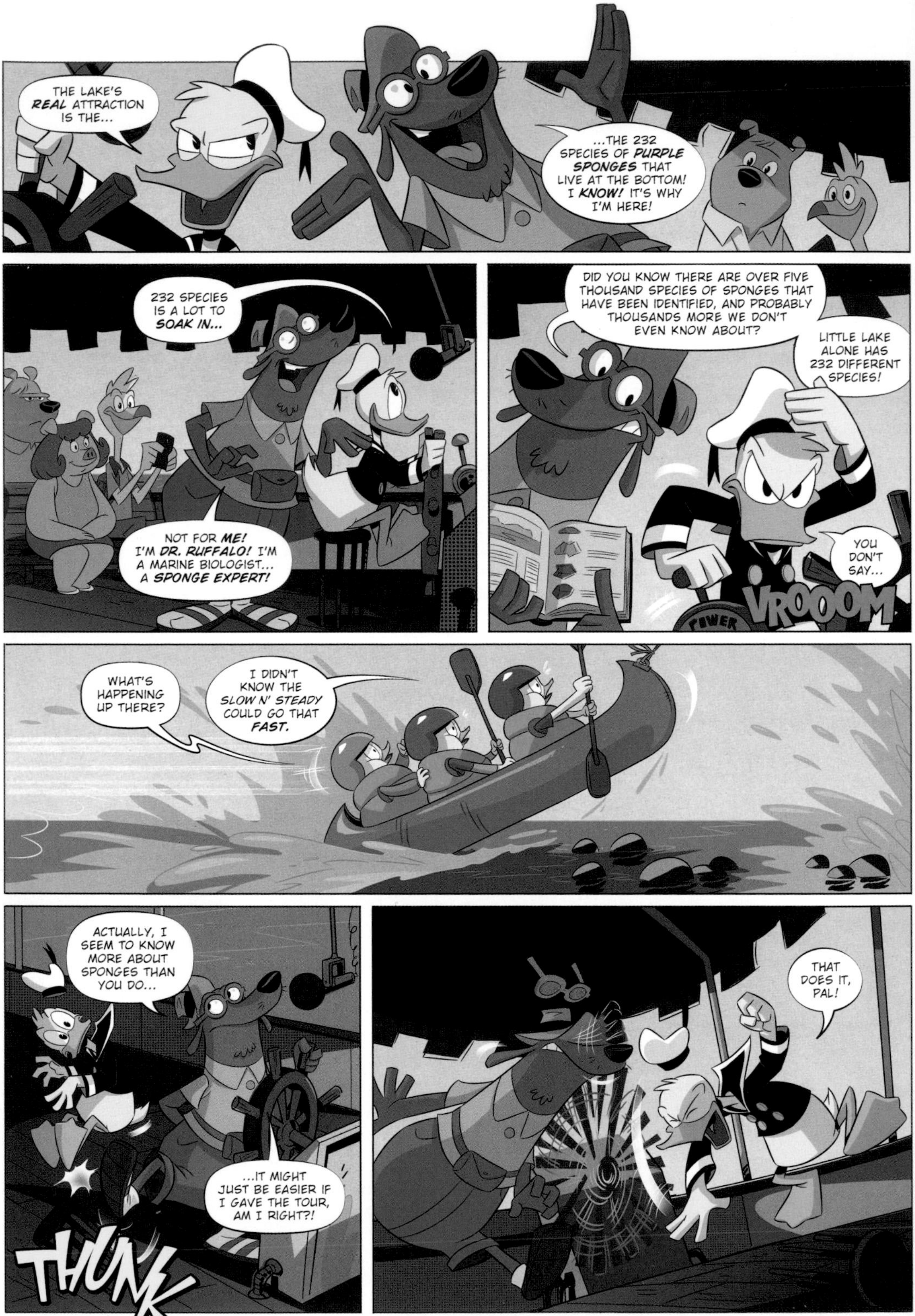
THE LAKE'S REAL ATTRACTION IS THE...
...THE 232 SPECIES OF PURPLE SPONGES THAT LIVE AT THE BOTTOM! I KNOW! IT'S WHY I'M HERE!
232 SPECIES IS A LOT TO SOAK IN...
NOT FOR ME! I'M DR. RUFFALO! I'M A MARINE BIOLOGIST... A SPONGE EXPERT!
DID YOU KNOW THERE ARE OVER FIVE THOUSAND SPECIES OF SPONGES THAT HAVE BEEN IDENTIFIED, AND PROBABLY THOUSANDS MORE WE DON'T EVEN KNOW ABOUT?
LITTLE LAKE ALONE HAS 232 DIFFERENT SPECIES!
YOU DON'T SAY...
POWER
VROOOM
WHAT'S HAPPENING UP THERE?
I DIDN'T KNOW THE SLOW N' STEADY COULD GO THAT FAST.
ACTUALLY, I SEEM TO KNOW MORE ABOUT SPONGES THAN YOU DO...
...IT MIGHT JUST BE EASIER IF I GAVE THE TOUR, AM I RIGHT?!
THUNK
THAT DOES IT, PAL!

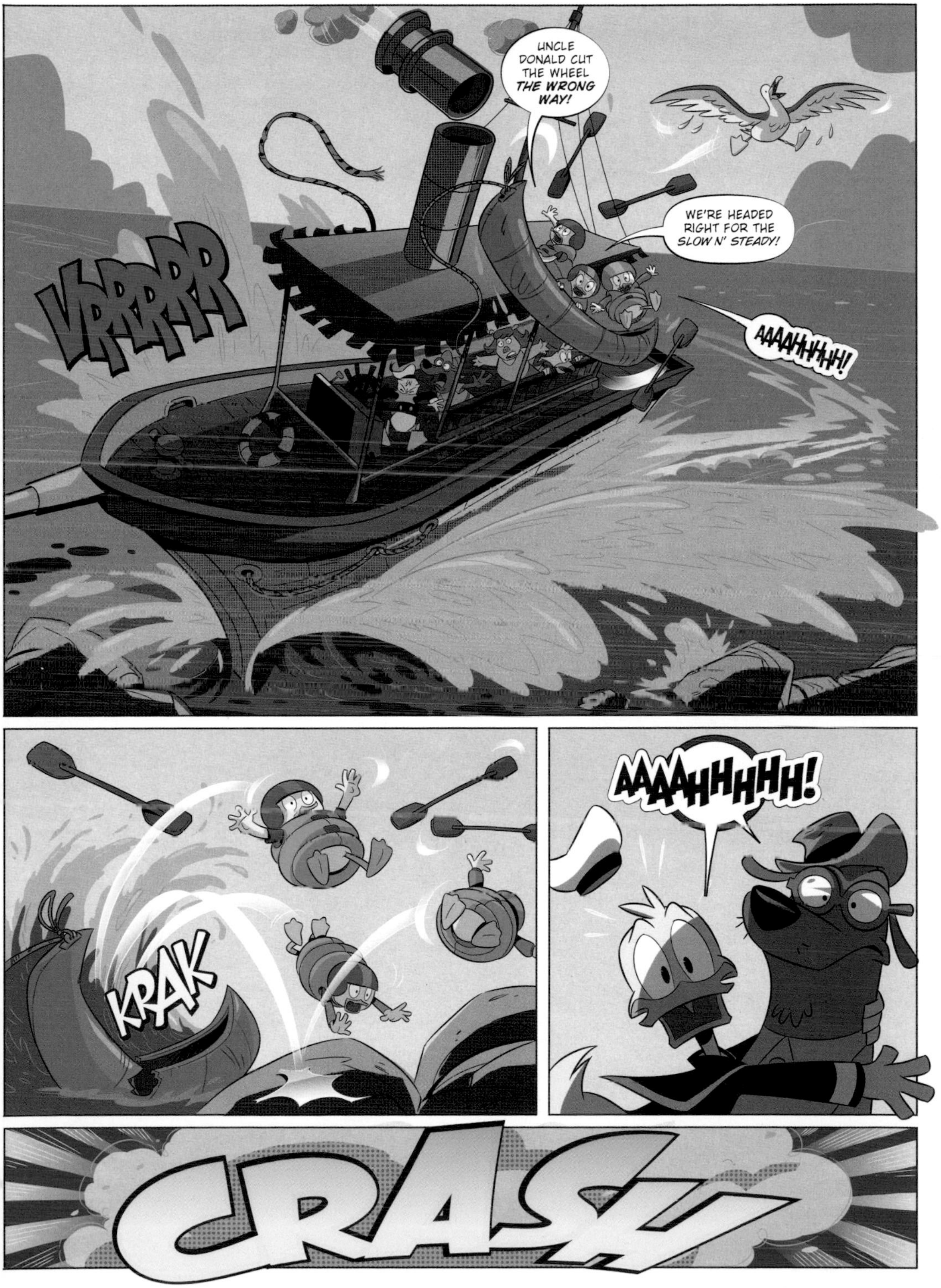
UNCLE DONALD CUT THE WHEEL *THE WRONG WAY!*
VRRRRR
WE'RE HEADED RIGHT FOR THE *SLOW N' STEADY!*
AAAAHHHHH!
KRAK
AAAAHHHHH!
CRASH

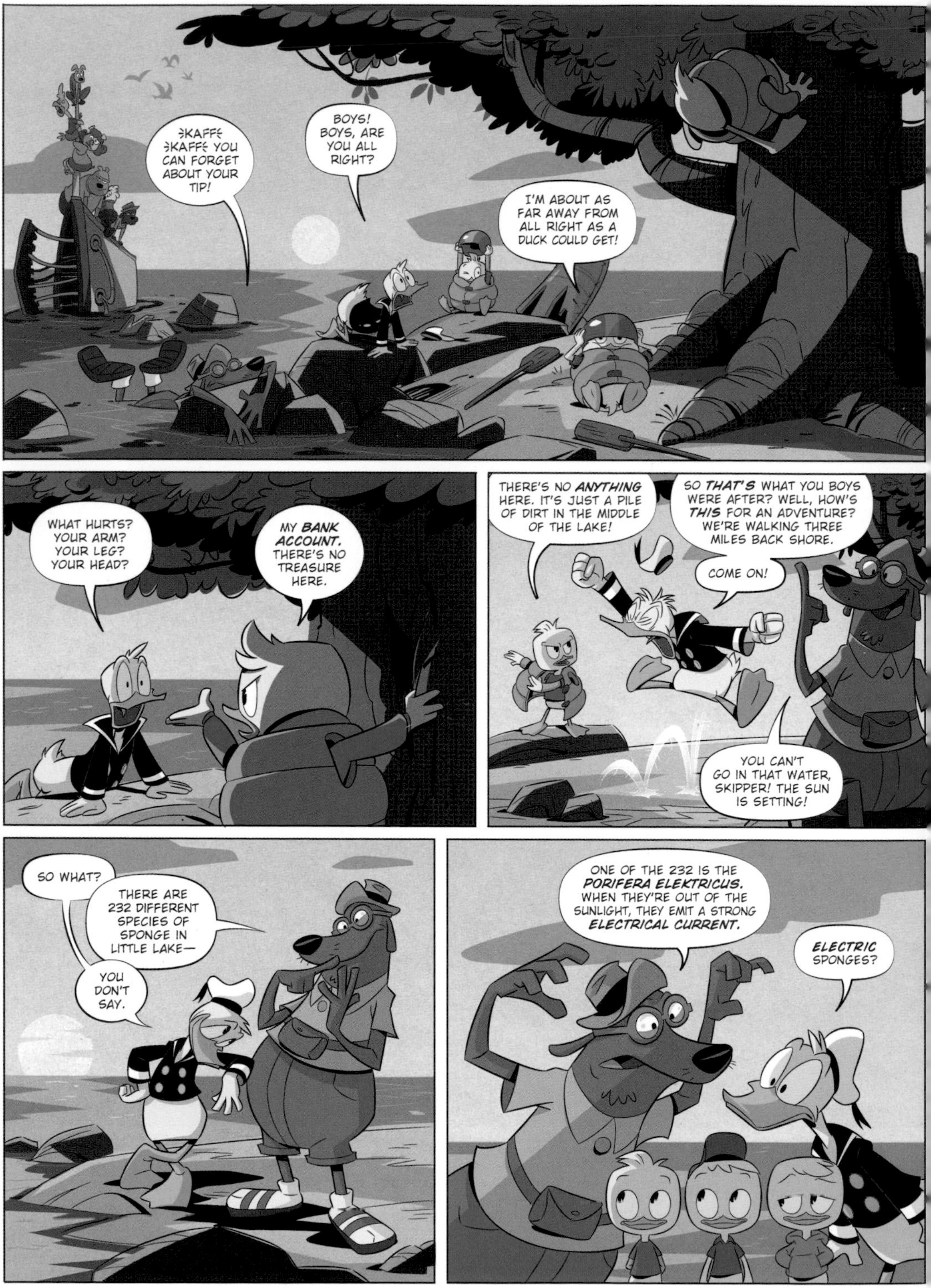

ƎKAFFƐ ƎKAFFƐ YOU CAN FORGET ABOUT YOUR TIP!
BOYS! BOYS, ARE YOU ALL RIGHT?
I'M ABOUT AS FAR AWAY FROM ALL RIGHT AS A DUCK COULD GET!
WHAT HURTS? YOUR ARM? YOUR LEG? YOUR HEAD?
MY BANK ACCOUNT. THERE'S NO TREASURE HERE.
THERE'S NO ANYTHING HERE. IT'S JUST A PILE OF DIRT IN THE MIDDLE OF THE LAKE!
SO THAT'S WHAT YOU BOYS WERE AFTER? WELL, HOW'S THIS FOR AN ADVENTURE? WE'RE WALKING THREE MILES BACK SHORE.
COME ON!
YOU CAN'T GO IN THAT WATER, SKIPPER! THE SUN IS SETTING!
SO WHAT?
THERE ARE 232 DIFFERENT SPECIES OF SPONGE IN LITTLE LAKE—
YOU DON'T SAY.
ONE OF THE 232 IS THE PORIFERA ELEKTRICUS. WHEN THEY'RE OUT OF THE SUNLIGHT, THEY EMIT A STRONG ELECTRICAL CURRENT.
ELECTRIC SPONGES?

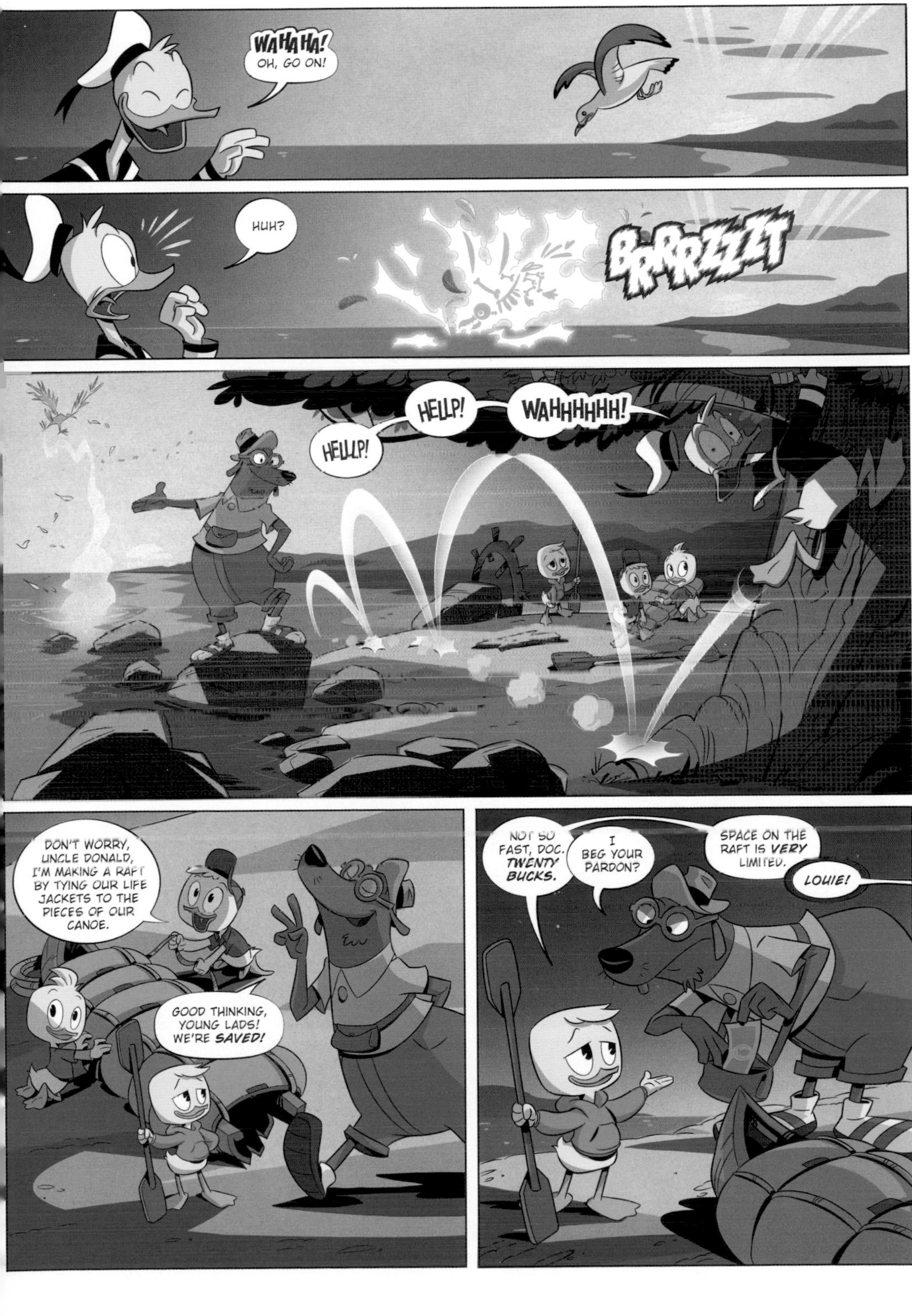
WAHAHA! OH, GO ON!
HUH?
BRRRZZZT
HELLLP!
HELLP!
WAHHHHHH!
DON'T WORRY, UNCLE DONALD, I'M MAKING A RAFT BY TYING OUR LIFE JACKETS TO THE PIECES OF OUR CANOE.
GOOD THINKING, YOUNG LADS! WE'RE SAVED!
NOT SO FAST, DOC. TWENTY BUCKS.
I BEG YOUR PARDON?
SPACE ON THE RAFT IS VERY LIMITED.
LOUIE!

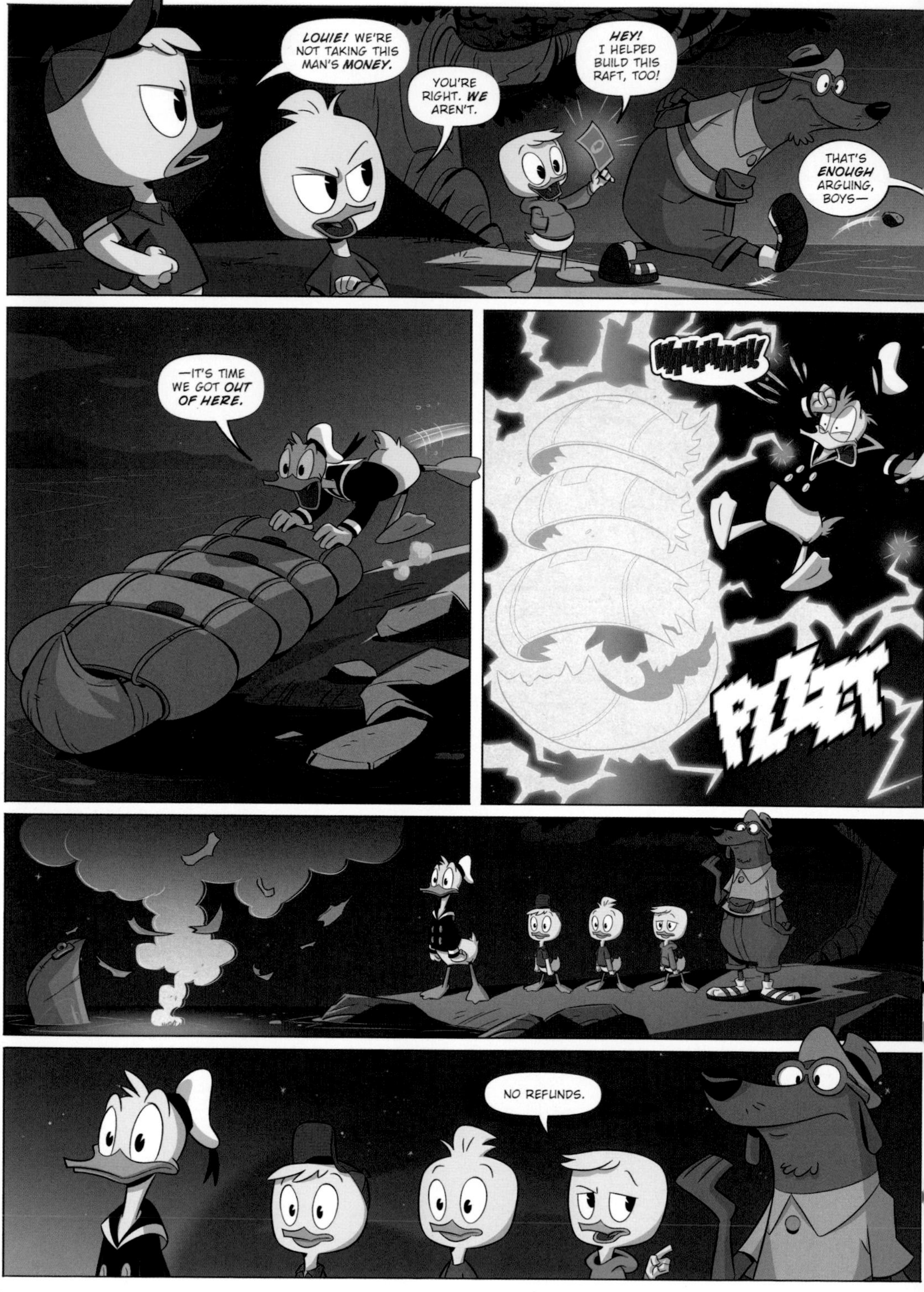
LOUIE! WE'RE NOT TAKING THIS MAN'S MONEY.
YOU'RE RIGHT. WE AREN'T.
HEY! I HELPED BUILD THIS RAFT, TOO!
THAT'S ENOUGH ARGUING, BOYS—
—IT'S TIME WE GOT OUT OF HERE.
PZZZT
NO REFUNDS.

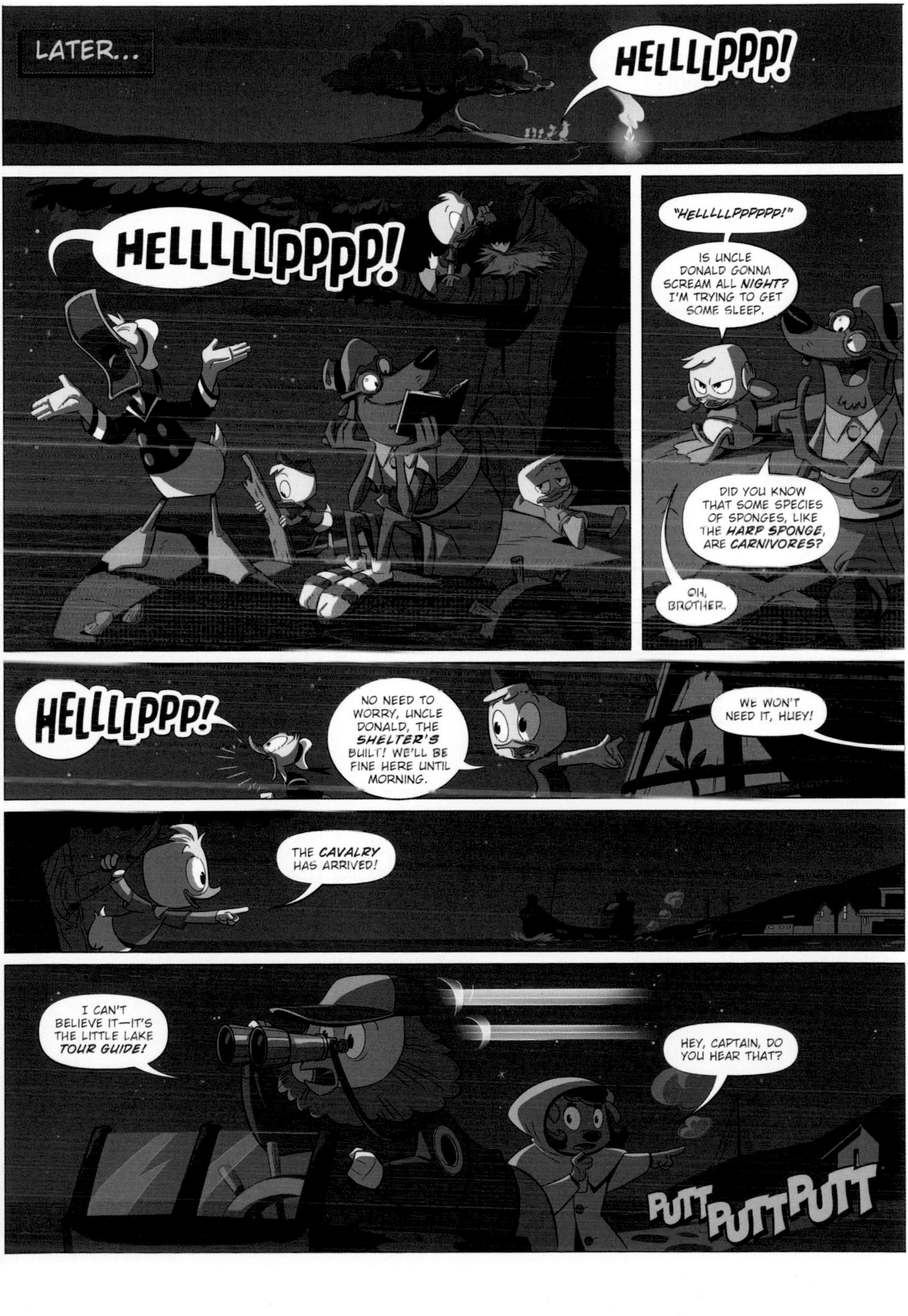
LATER...
HELLLLPPP!
HELLLLLPPPP!
"HELLLLLLPPPPPP!"
IS UNCLE DONALD GONNA SCREAM ALL NIGHT? I'M TRYING TO GET SOME SLEEP.
DID YOU KNOW THAT SOME SPECIES OF SPONGES, LIKE THE HARP SPONGE, ARE CARNIVORES?
OH, BROTHER.
HELLLLPPP!
NO NEED TO WORRY, UNCLE DONALD, THE SHELTER'S BUILT! WE'LL BE FINE HERE UNTIL MORNING.
WE WON'T NEED IT, HUEY!
THE CAVALRY HAS ARRIVED!
I CAN'T BELIEVE IT—IT'S THE LITTLE LAKE TOUR GUIDE!
HEY, CAPTAIN, DO YOU HEAR THAT?
PUTT PUTT PUTT

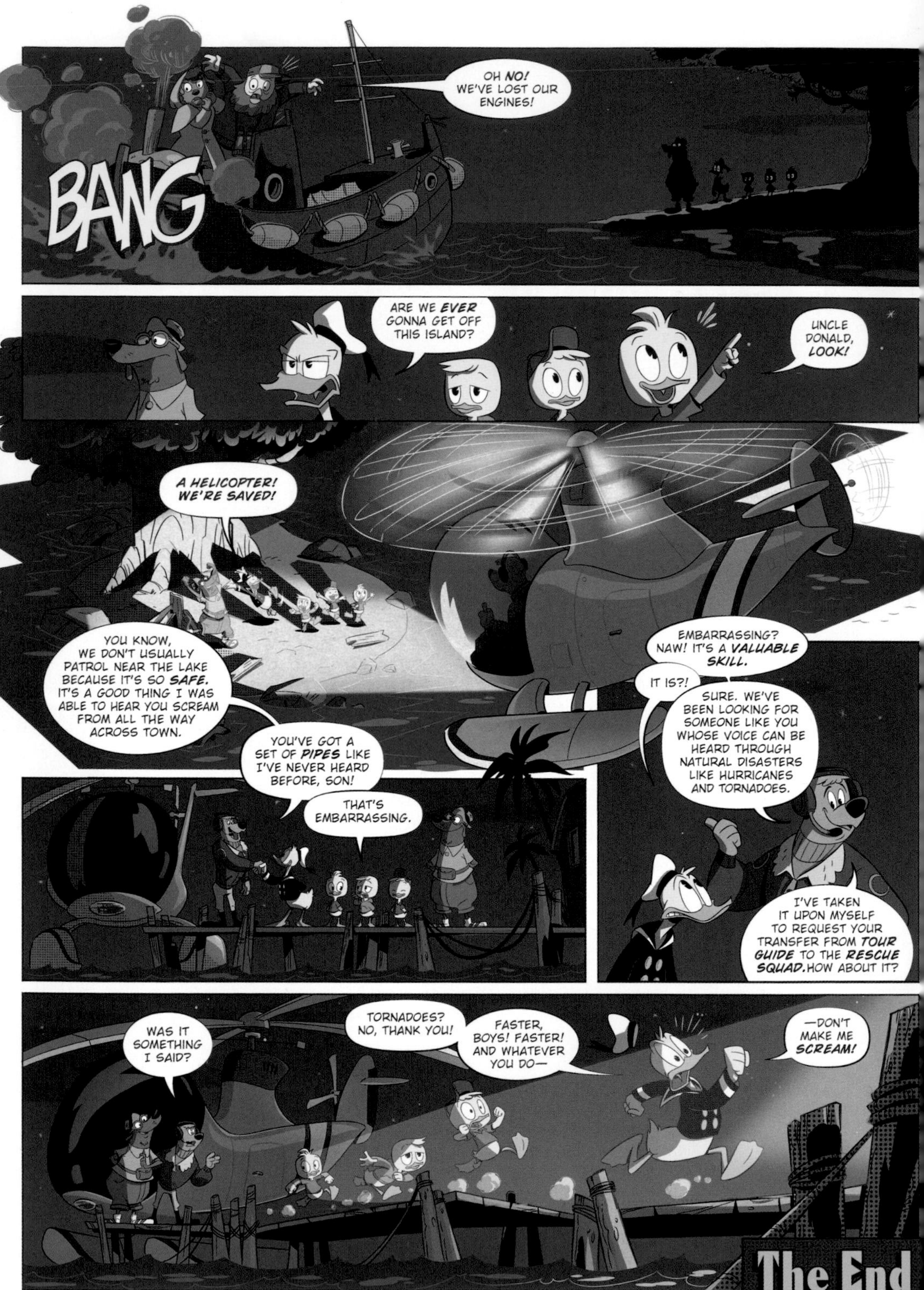
BANG
OH NO! WE'VE LOST OUR ENGINES!
ARE WE EVER GONNA GET OFF THIS ISLAND?
UNCLE DONALD, LOOK!
A HELICOPTER! WE'RE SAVED!
YOU KNOW, WE DON'T USUALLY PATROL NEAR THE LAKE BECAUSE IT'S SO SAFE. IT'S A GOOD THING I WAS ABLE TO HEAR YOU SCREAM FROM ALL THE WAY ACROSS TOWN.
YOU'VE GOT A SET OF PIPES LIKE I'VE NEVER HEARD BEFORE, SON!
THAT'S EMBARRASSING.
EMBARRASSING? NAW! IT'S A VALUABLE SKILL.
IT IS?!
SURE. WE'VE BEEN LOOKING FOR SOMEONE LIKE YOU WHOSE VOICE CAN BE HEARD THROUGH NATURAL DISASTERS LIKE HURRICANES AND TORNADOES.
I'VE TAKEN IT UPON MYSELF TO REQUEST YOUR TRANSFER FROM TOUR GUIDE TO THE RESCUE SQUAD. HOW ABOUT IT?
WAS IT SOMETHING I SAID?
TORNADOES? NO, THANK YOU!
FASTER, BOYS! FASTER! AND WHATEVER YOU DO—
—DON'T MAKE ME SCREAM!
The End

THE REPEATING REVENGE OF THE SCREAMING DUCK!

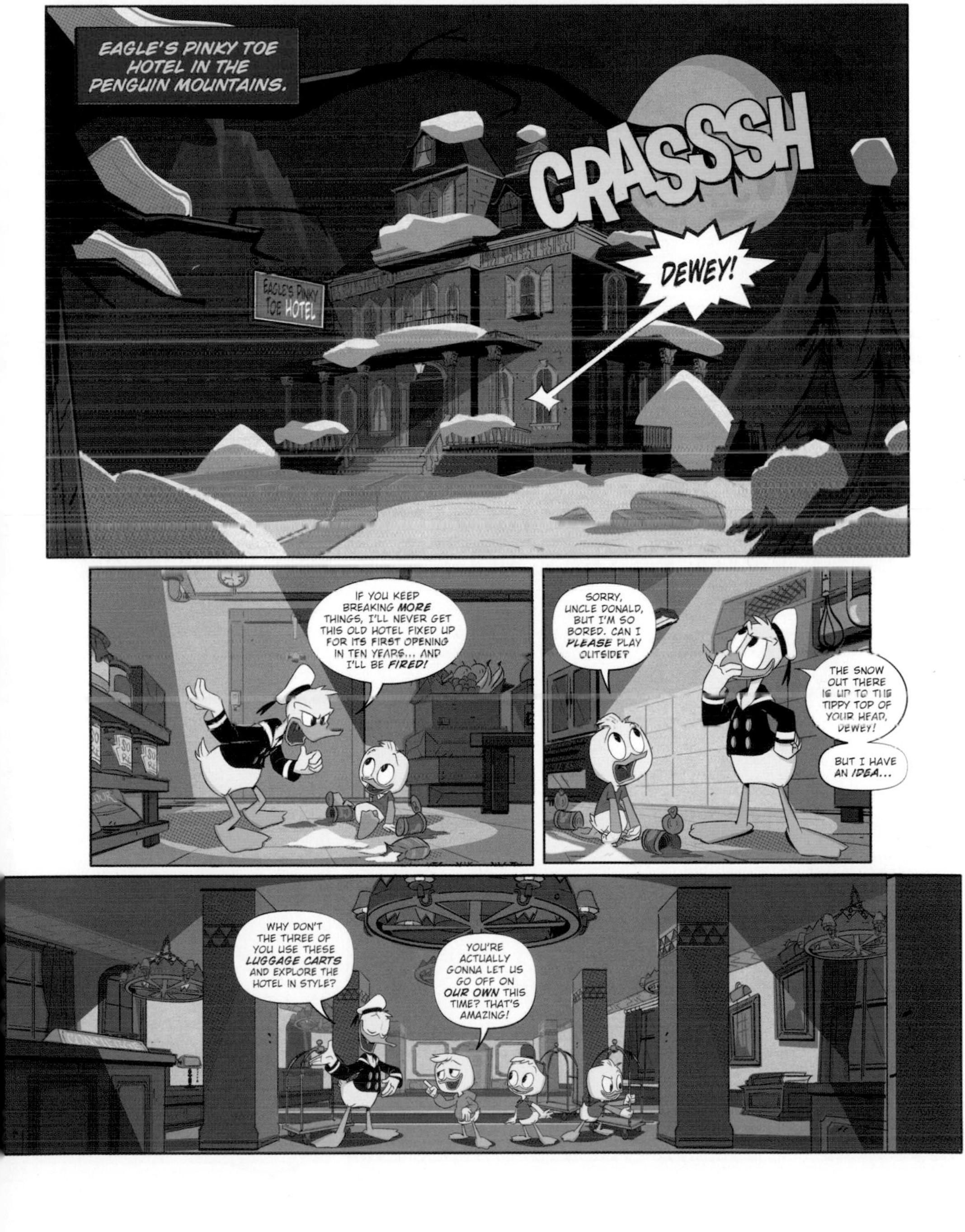
EAGLE'S PINKY TOE HOTEL IN THE PENGUIN MOUNTAINS.
CRASSSH
EAGLE'S PINKY TOE HOTEL
DEWEY!
IF YOU KEEP BREAKING MORE THINGS, I'LL NEVER GET THIS OLD HOTEL FIXED UP FOR ITS FIRST OPENING IN TEN YEARS... AND I'LL BE FIRED!
SORRY, UNCLE DONALD, BUT I'M SO BORED. CAN I PLEASE PLAY OUTSIDE?
THE SNOW OUT THERE IS UP TO THE TIPPY TOP OF YOUR HEAD, DEWEY!
BUT I HAVE AN IDEA...
WHY DON'T THE THREE OF YOU USE THESE LUGGAGE CARTS AND EXPLORE THE HOTEL IN STYLE?
YOU'RE ACTUALLY GONNA LET US GO OFF ON OUR OWN THIS TIME? THAT'S AMAZING!

OF *COURSE* NOT! I'VE ATTACHED A *GPS* UNIT TO EACH ONE SO THEY CAN BE TRACKED AT ANY TIME.

NOT SO AMAZING.

BUT *BRILLIANT!* NOW HOTEL MANAGEMENT CAN KEEP TRACK OF PEOPLE'S LUGGAGE!

UH, YEAH... SURE... *THAT'S* WHAT IT'S FOR.

WHO CARES? I'M OUTTA HERE BEFORE UNCLE DONALD CHANGES HIS MIND!

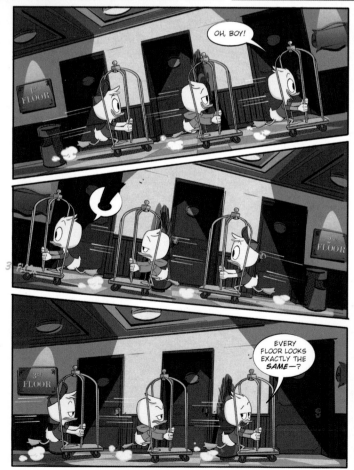

OH, BOY!

1st FLOOR

2nd FLOOR

3rd FLOOR

EVERY FLOOR LOOKS EXACTLY THE *SAME*—?

AAAIINEEEEEEEE!

DEWEY, ARE YOU ALL RIGHT?

THE LAST TIME I HEARD A DUCK *SCREAM* LIKE THAT WAS—

IT WASN'T *ME*, LOUIE, IT—IT CAME FROM... IN *THERE!*

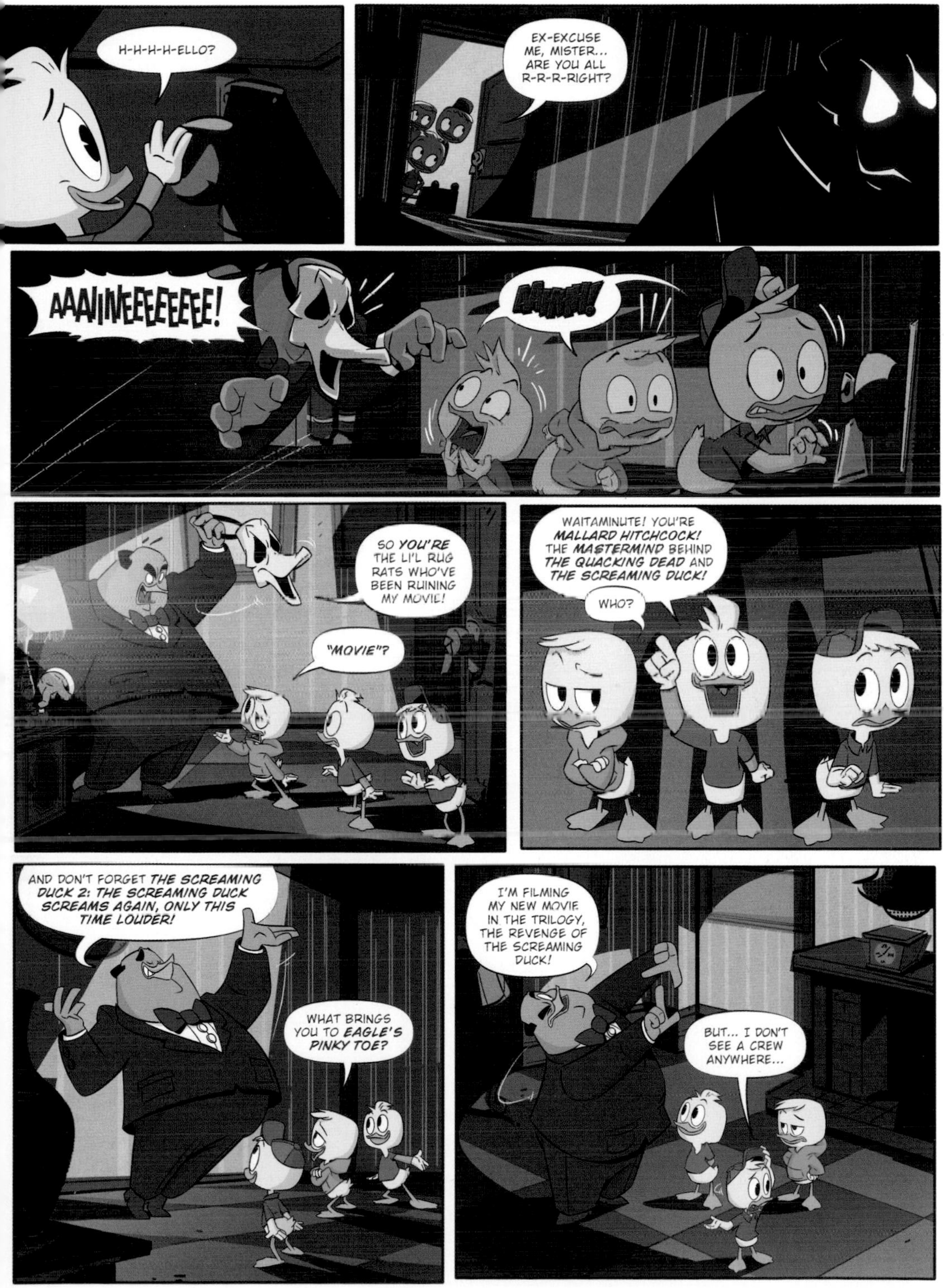
H-H-H-H-ELLO?
EX-EXCUSE ME, MISTER... ARE YOU ALL R-R-R-RIGHT?
AAAIINEEEEEEEE!
SO YOU'RE THE LI'L RUG RATS WHO'VE BEEN RUINING MY MOVIE!
"MOVIE"?
WAITAMINUTE! YOU'RE MALLARD HITCHCOCK! THE MASTERMIND BEHIND THE QUACKING DEAD AND THE SCREAMING DUCK!
WHO?
AND DON'T FORGET THE SCREAMING DUCK 2: THE SCREAMING DUCK SCREAMS AGAIN, ONLY THIS TIME LOUDER!
WHAT BRINGS YOU TO EAGLE'S PINKY TOE?
I'M FILMING MY NEW MOVIE IN THE TRILOGY, THE REVENGE OF THE SCREAMING DUCK!
BUT... I DON'T SEE A CREW ANYWHERE...

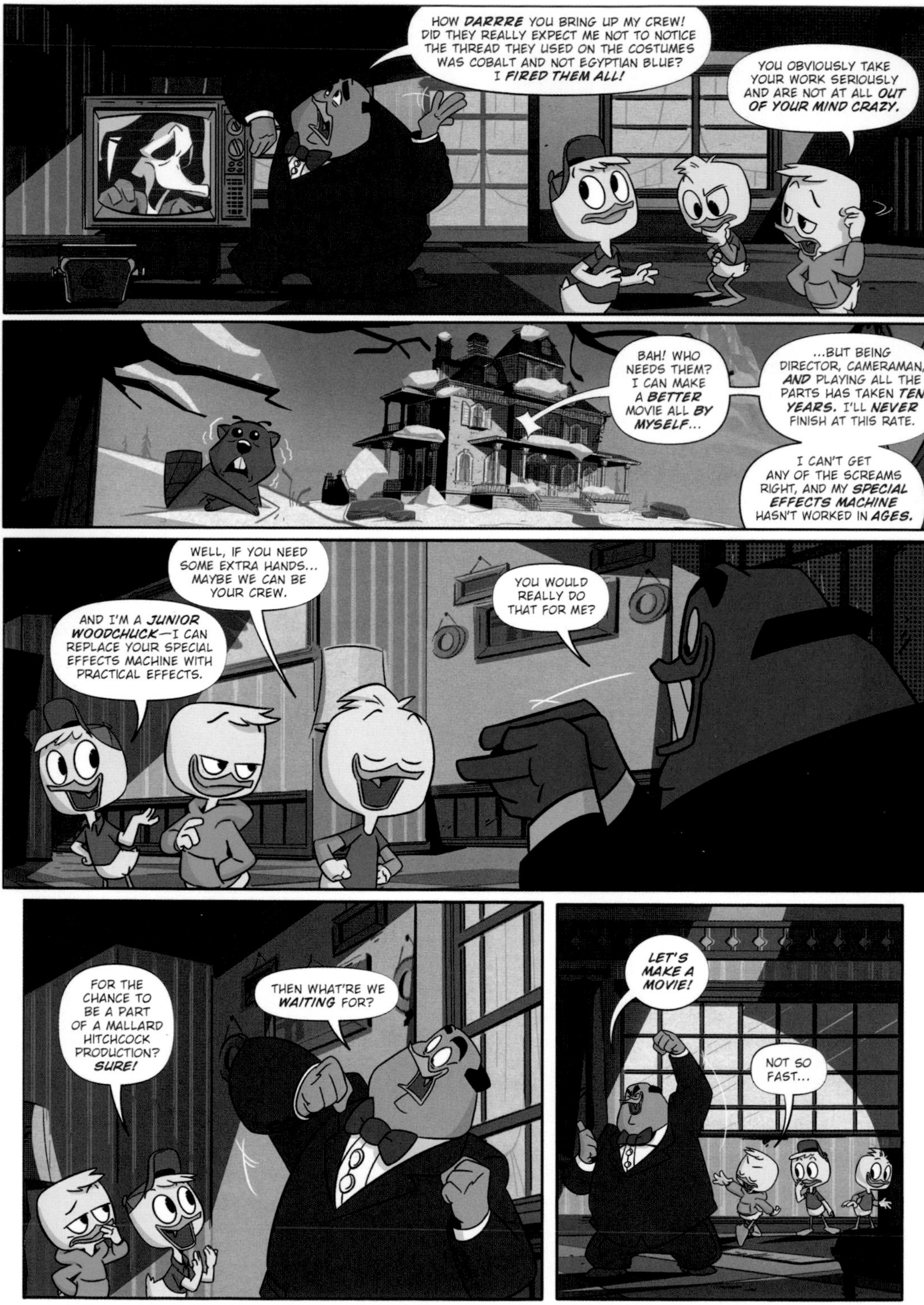

HOW DARRRE YOU BRING UP MY CREW! DID THEY REALLY EXPECT ME NOT TO NOTICE THE THREAD THEY USED ON THE COSTUMES WAS COBALT AND NOT EGYPTIAN BLUE? I FIRED THEM ALL!
YOU OBVIOUSLY TAKE YOUR WORK SERIOUSLY AND ARE NOT AT ALL OUT OF YOUR MIND CRAZY.
BAH! WHO NEEDS THEM? I CAN MAKE A BETTER MOVIE ALL BY MYSELF...
...BUT BEING DIRECTOR, CAMERAMAN, AND PLAYING ALL THE PARTS HAS TAKEN TEN YEARS. I'LL NEVER FINISH AT THIS RATE.
I CAN'T GET ANY OF THE SCREAMS RIGHT, AND MY SPECIAL EFFECTS MACHINE HASN'T WORKED IN AGES.
WELL, IF YOU NEED SOME EXTRA HANDS... MAYBE WE CAN BE YOUR CREW.
AND I'M A JUNIOR WOODCHUCK—I CAN REPLACE YOUR SPECIAL EFFECTS MACHINE WITH PRACTICAL EFFECTS.
YOU WOULD REALLY DO THAT FOR ME?
FOR THE CHANCE TO BE A PART OF A MALLARD HITCHCOCK PRODUCTION? SURE!
THEN WHAT'RE WE WAITING FOR?
LET'S MAKE A MOVIE!
NOT SO FAST...

WHO'S GOING TO BE THE **SCREAMING DUCK?**

ME, OF COURSE!

BUT YOU SAID ACTING AND DIRECTING WAS TAKING TOO LONG. IF I MAY...

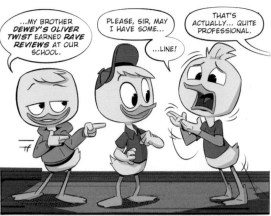

...MY BROTHER **DEWEY'S** OLIVER **TW!ST** EARNED **RAVE REVIEWS** AT OUR SCHOOL.

PLEASE, SIR, MAY I HAVE SOME...

...LINE!

THAT'S ACTUALLY... QUITE PROFESSIONAL.

SO YOU'LL **PAY** HIM, THEN?

I'LL PAY HIM **SCALE** AND NOT A **PENNY** MORE!

I GUESS THAT'LL DO... AS LONG AS THE **UNION** DOESN'T FIND OUT HE'S ALSO DOING HIS OWN STUNTS...

RRRRRR--**FINE!** I'LL PAY HIM **ONE AND A HALF** TIMES SCALE BUT **THAT'S IT!**... I THOUGHT YOU BOYS WERE FANS.

TO BE FAIR, I WAS FAMILIAR WITH MONEY'S WORK LONG BEFORE I KNEW ABOUT YOURS.

BY THE WAY, YOU OWE ME **TWENTY PERCENT.**

LATER...

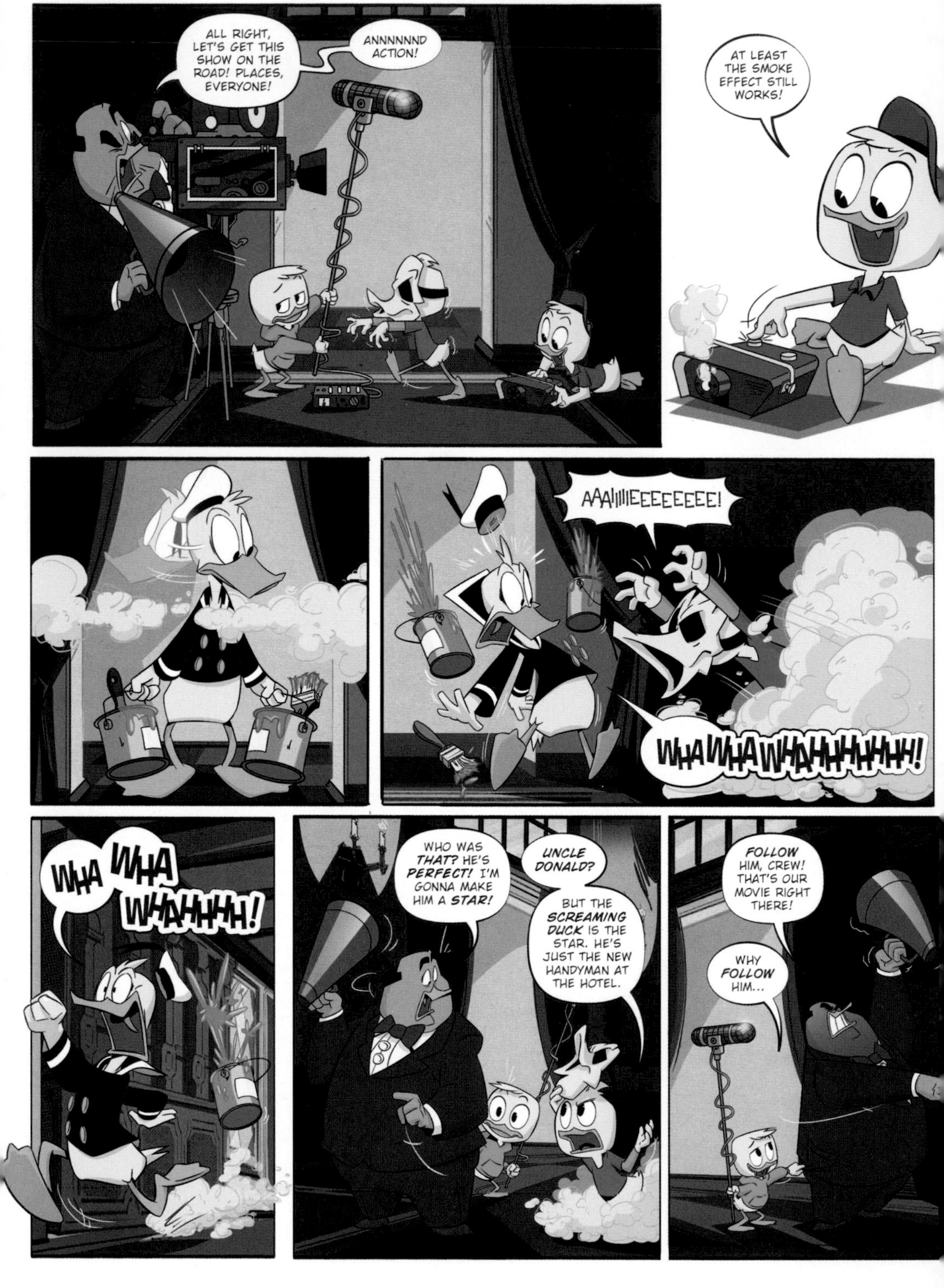
ALL RIGHT, LET'S GET THIS SHOW ON THE ROAD! PLACES, EVERYONE!
ANNNNNND ACTION!
AT LEAST THE SMOKE EFFECT STILL WORKS!
AAAIIIIIEEEEEEEE!
WHAWHAWHAHHHHHH!
WHA WHA WHAHHHH!
WHO WAS THAT? HE'S PERFECT! I'M GONNA MAKE HIM A STAR!
UNCLE DONALD?
BUT THE SCREAMING DUCK IS THE STAR. HE'S JUST THE NEW HANDYMAN AT THE HOTEL.
FOLLOW HIM, CREW! THAT'S OUR MOVIE RIGHT THERE!
WHY FOLLOW HIM...

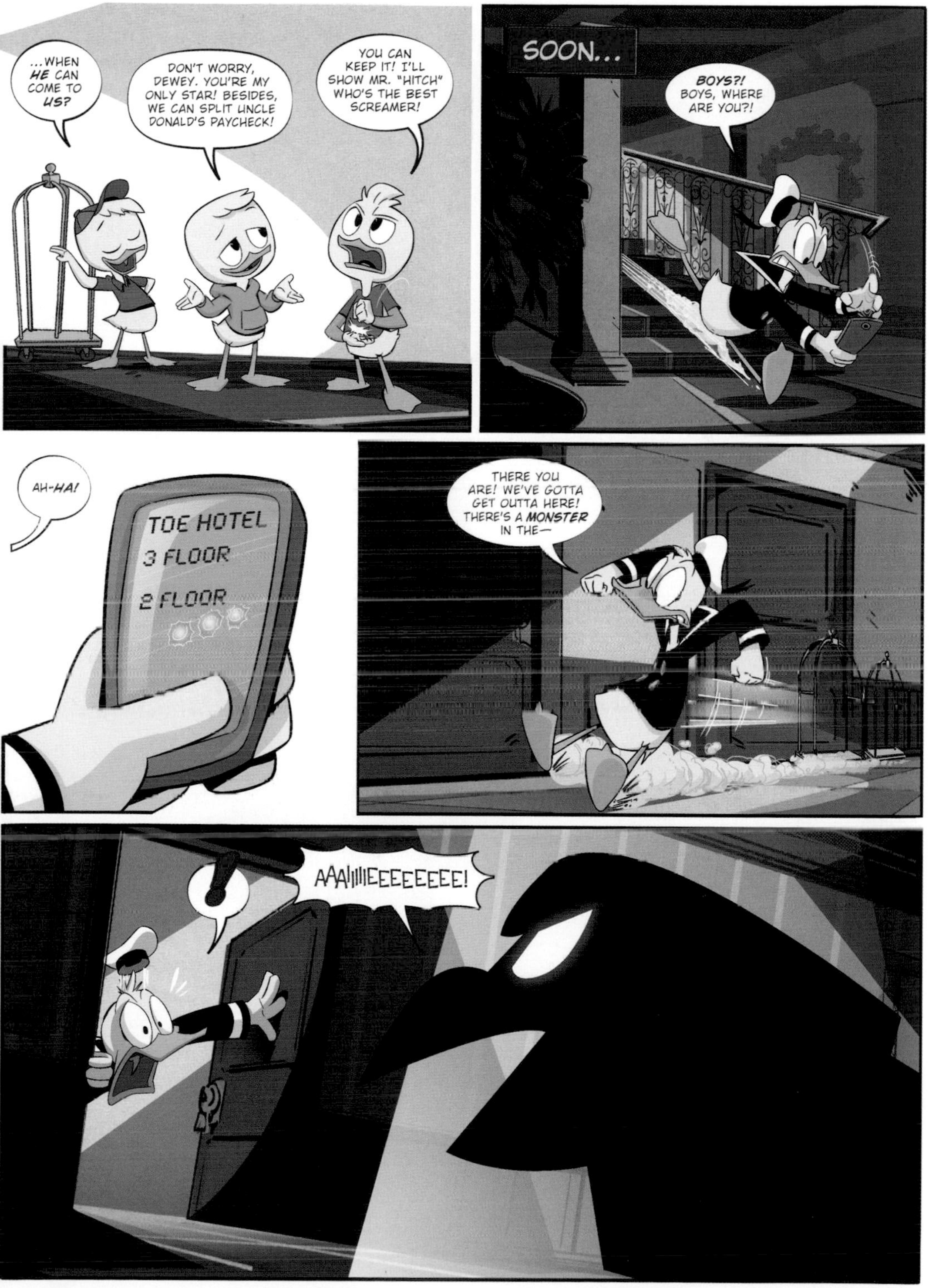
...WHEN HE CAN COME TO US?
DON'T WORRY, DEWEY. YOU'RE MY ONLY STAR! BESIDES, WE CAN SPLIT UNCLE DONALD'S PAYCHECK!
YOU CAN KEEP IT! I'LL SHOW MR. "HITCH" WHO'S THE BEST SCREAMER!
SOON...
BOYS?! BOYS, WHERE ARE YOU?!
AH-HA!
TOE HOTEL
3 FLOOR
2 FLOOR
THERE YOU ARE! WE'VE GOTTA GET OUTTA HERE! THERE'S A MONSTER IN THE—
AAAIIIIIEEEEEEEE!

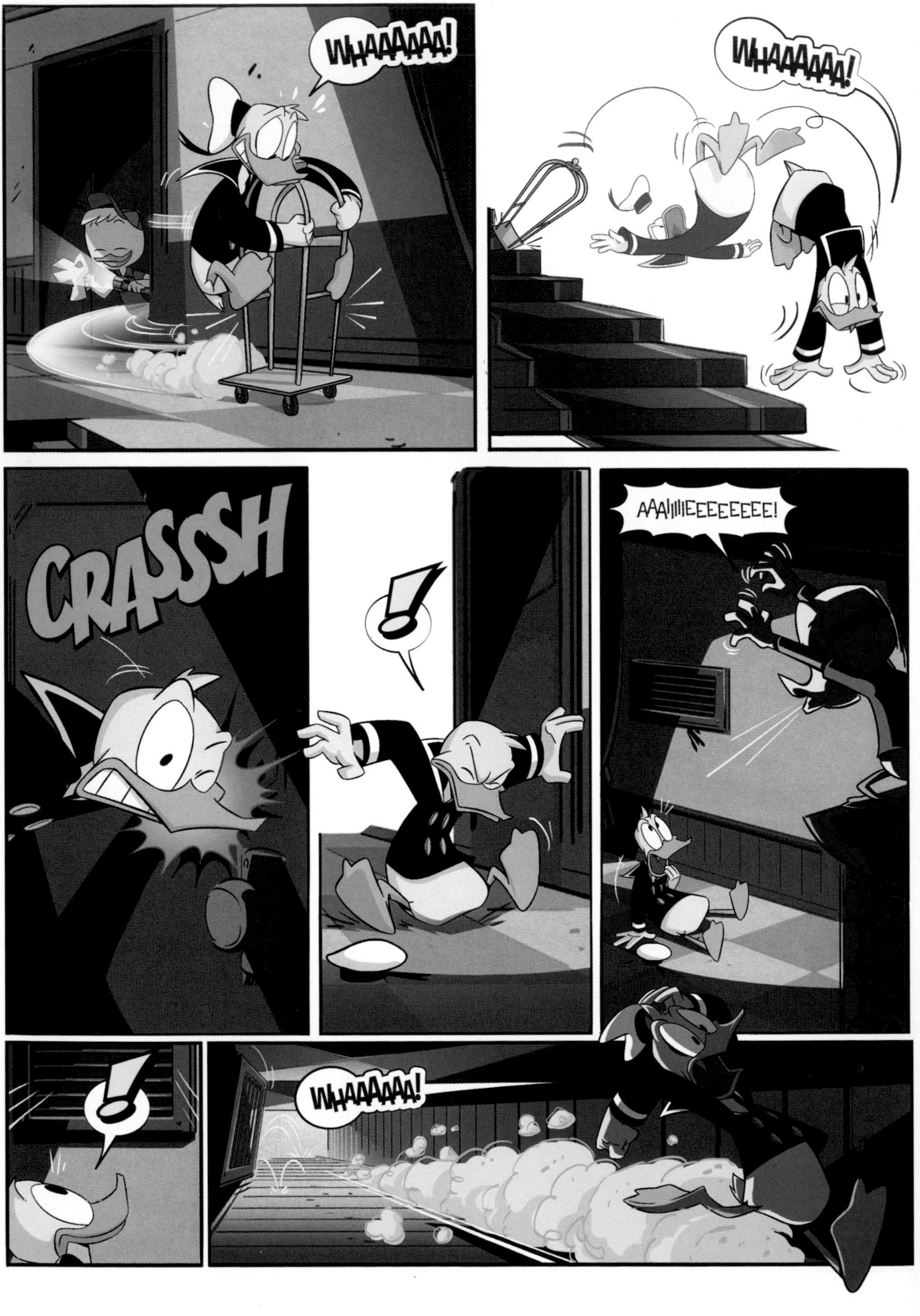

WHAAAAAA!
WHAAAAAAA!
CRASSSH
!
AAAIIIIIEEEEEEEE!
!
WHAAAAAA!

BEEP B-DEEP!

2 LUGGAGE CARTS NEARBY

BEEP BEEP B-DEEP!

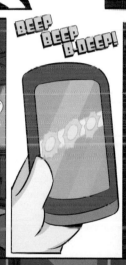

WHAAAAAA!

WHAAAAAA!

UNCLE DONALD! HELLLLLLP!

HEEEEERE'S MALLARD!

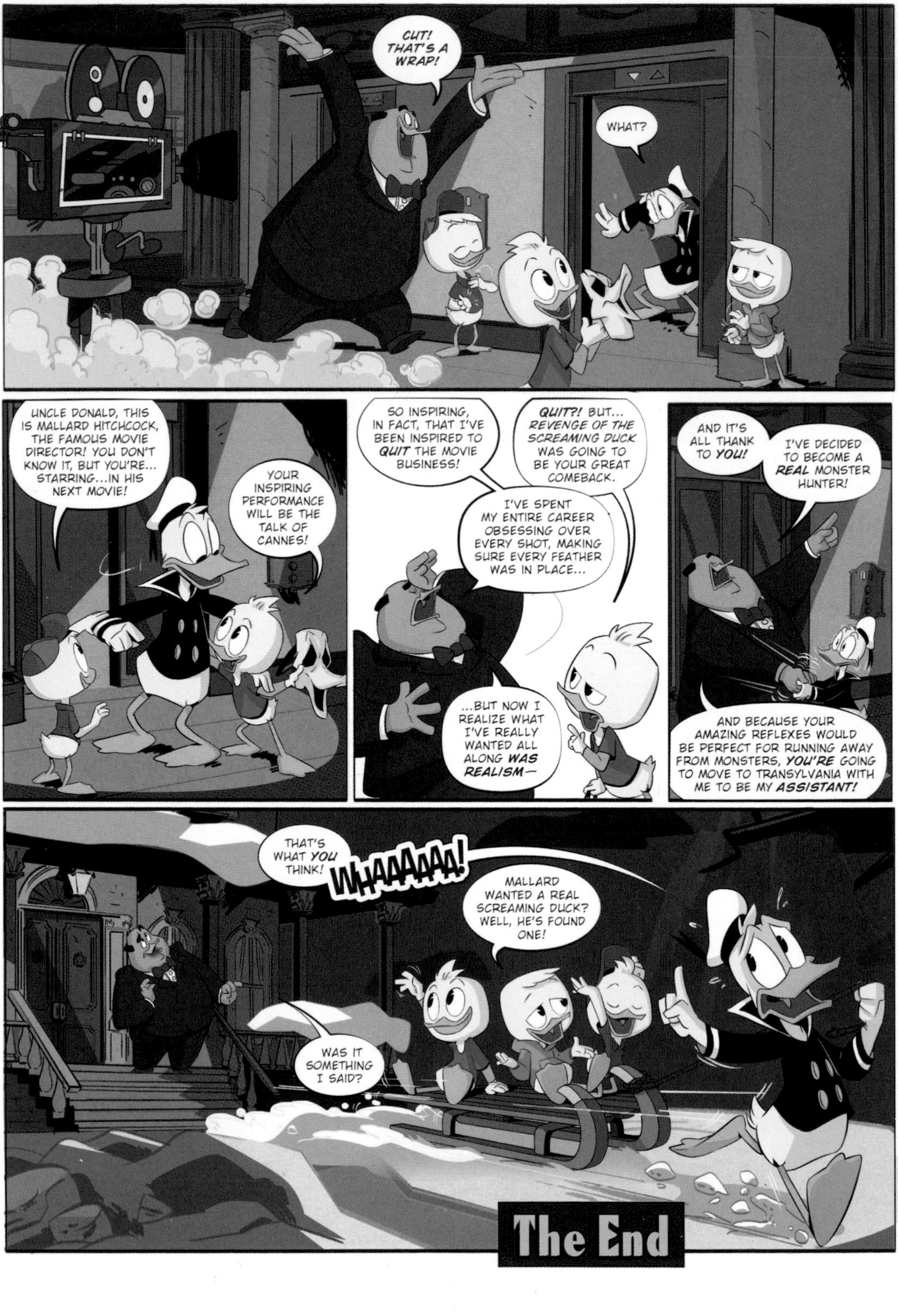
CUT! THAT'S A WRAP!
WHAT?
UNCLE DONALD, THIS IS MALLARD HITCHCOCK, THE FAMOUS MOVIE DIRECTOR! YOU DON'T KNOW IT, BUT YOU'RE... STARRING...IN HIS NEXT MOVIE!
YOUR INSPIRING PERFORMANCE WILL BE THE TALK OF CANNES!
SO INSPIRING, IN FACT, THAT I'VE BEEN INSPIRED TO QUIT THE MOVIE BUSINESS!
QUIT?! BUT... REVENGE OF THE SCREAMING DUCK WAS GOING TO BE YOUR GREAT COMEBACK.
I'VE SPENT MY ENTIRE CAREER OBSESSING OVER EVERY SHOT, MAKING SURE EVERY FEATHER WAS IN PLACE...
...BUT NOW I REALIZE WHAT I'VE REALLY WANTED ALL ALONG WAS REALISM—
AND IT'S ALL THANK TO YOU!
I'VE DECIDED TO BECOME A REAL MONSTER HUNTER!
AND BECAUSE YOUR AMAZING REFLEXES WOULD BE PERFECT FOR RUNNING AWAY FROM MONSTERS, YOU'RE GOING TO MOVE TO TRANSYLVANIA WITH ME TO BE MY ASSISTANT!
THAT'S WHAT YOU THINK!
WHAAAAAA!
MALLARD WANTED A REAL SCREAMING DUCK? WELL, HE'S FOUND ONE!
WAS IT SOMETHING I SAID?
The End

Disney DuckTales

THE CHILLING SECRET OF THE LIGHTHOUSE!

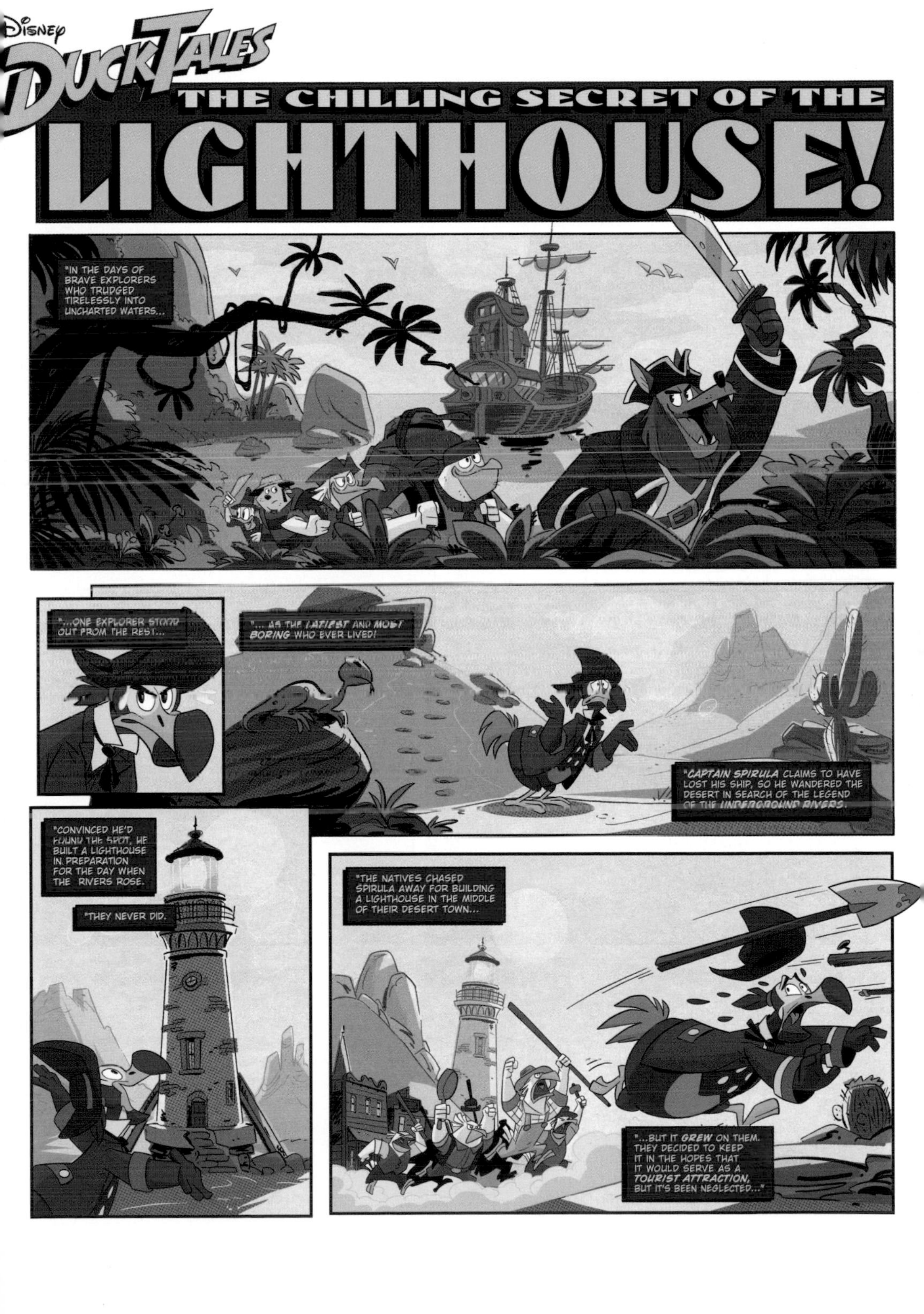
"IN THE DAYS OF BRAVE EXPLORERS WHO TRUDGED TIRELESSLY INTO UNCHARTED WATERS...
"...ONE EXPLORER STOOD OUT FROM THE REST...
"... AS THE LAZIEST AND MOST BORING WHO EVER LIVED!
"CAPTAIN SPIRULA CLAIMS TO HAVE LOST HIS SHIP, SO HE WANDERED THE DESERT IN SEARCH OF THE LEGEND OF THE UNDERGROUND RIVERS.
"CONVINCED HE'D FOUND THE SPOT, HE BUILT A LIGHTHOUSE IN PREPARATION FOR THE DAY WHEN THE RIVERS ROSE.
"THEY NEVER DID.
"THE NATIVES CHASED SPIRULA AWAY FOR BUILDING A LIGHTHOUSE IN THE MIDDLE OF THEIR DESERT TOWN...
"...BUT IT GREW ON THEM. THEY DECIDED TO KEEP IT IN THE HOPES THAT IT WOULD SERVE AS A TOURIST ATTRACTION, BUT IT'S BEEN NEGLECTED..."

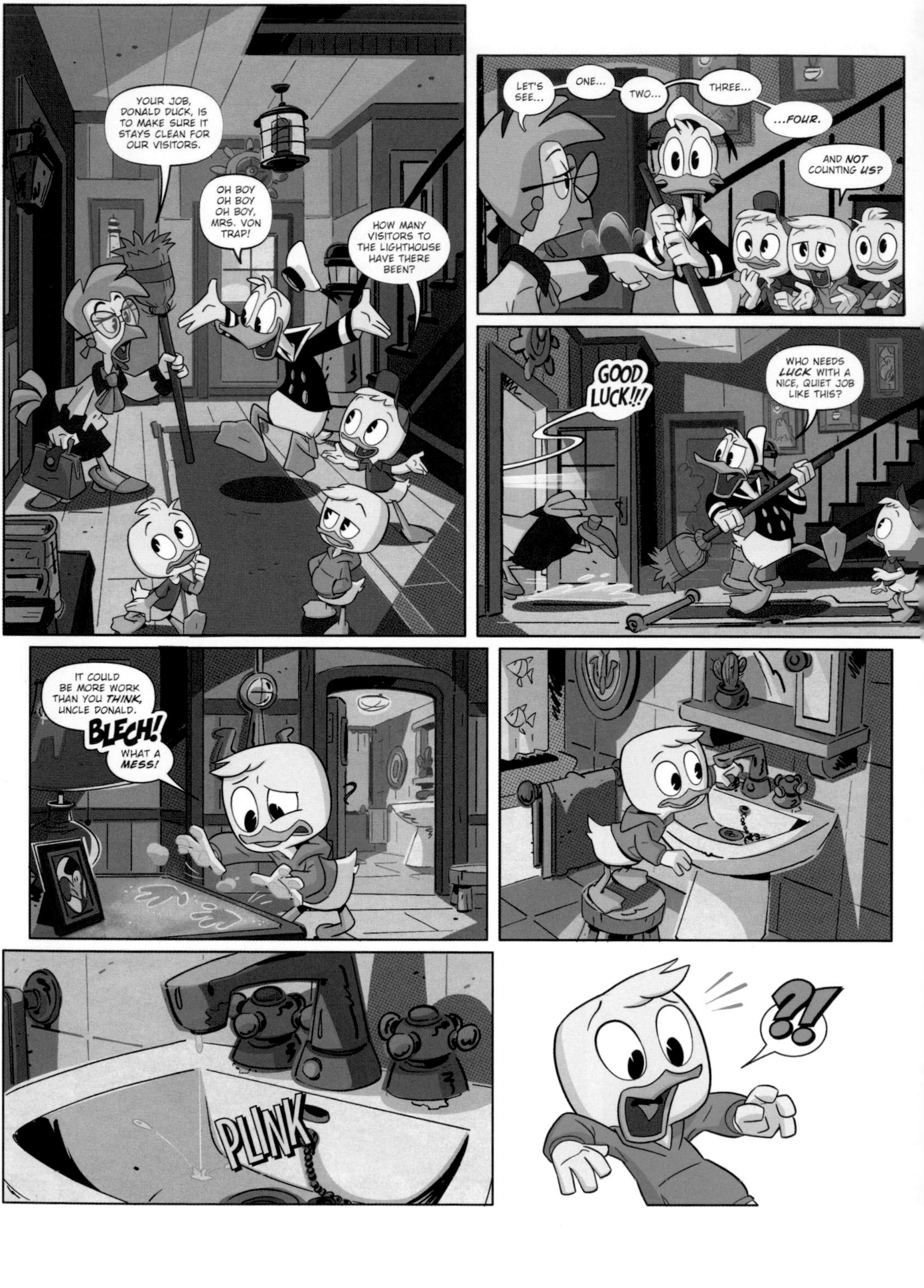
YOUR JOB, DONALD DUCK, IS TO MAKE SURE IT STAYS CLEAN FOR OUR VISITORS.
OH BOY OH BOY OH BOY, MRS. VON TRAP!
HOW MANY VISITORS TO THE LIGHTHOUSE HAVE THERE BEEN?
LET'S SEE...
ONE...
TWO...
THREE...
...FOUR.
AND NOT COUNTING US?
GOOD LUCK!!!
WHO NEEDS LUCK WITH A NICE, QUIET JOB LIKE THIS?
IT COULD BE MORE WORK THAN YOU THINK, UNCLE DONALD.
BLECH!
WHAT A MESS!
PLINK
?!

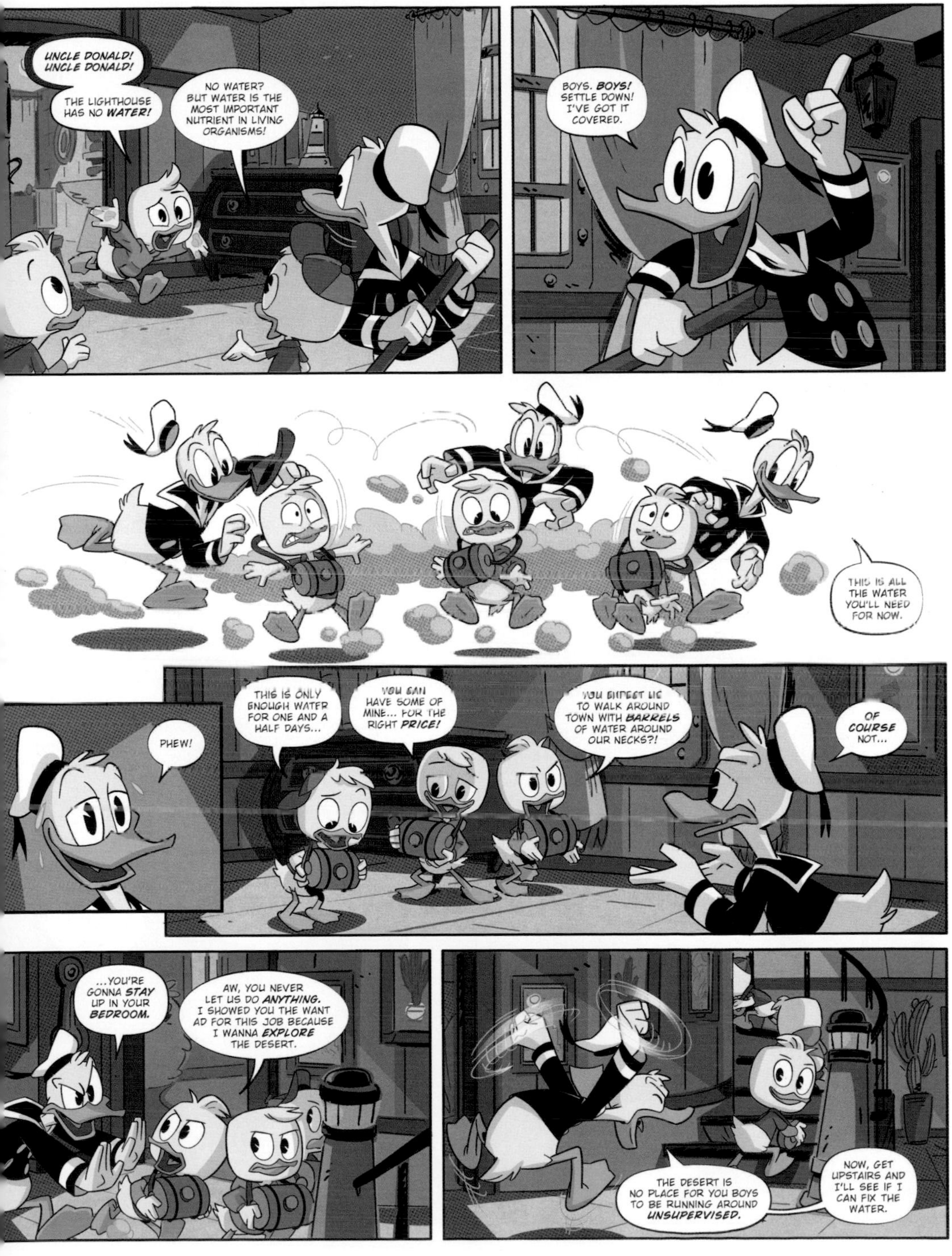
UNCLE DONALD! UNCLE DONALD!
THE LIGHTHOUSE HAS NO WATER!
NO WATER? BUT WATER IS THE MOST IMPORTANT NUTRIENT IN LIVING ORGANISMS!
BOYS. BOYS! SETTLE DOWN! I'VE GOT IT COVERED.
THIS IS ALL THE WATER YOU'LL NEED FOR NOW.
PHEW!
THIS IS ONLY ENOUGH WATER FOR ONE AND A HALF DAYS...
YOU CAN HAVE SOME OF MINE... FOR THE RIGHT PRICE!
YOU EXPECT US TO WALK AROUND TOWN WITH BARRELS OF WATER AROUND OUR NECKS?!
OF COURSE NOT...
...YOU'RE GONNA STAY UP IN YOUR BEDROOM.
AW, YOU NEVER LET US DO ANYTHING. I SHOWED YOU THE WANT AD FOR THIS JOB BECAUSE I WANNA EXPLORE THE DESERT.
THE DESERT IS NO PLACE FOR YOU BOYS TO BE RUNNING AROUND UNSUPERVISED.
NOW, GET UPSTAIRS AND I'LL SEE IF I CAN FIX THE WATER.

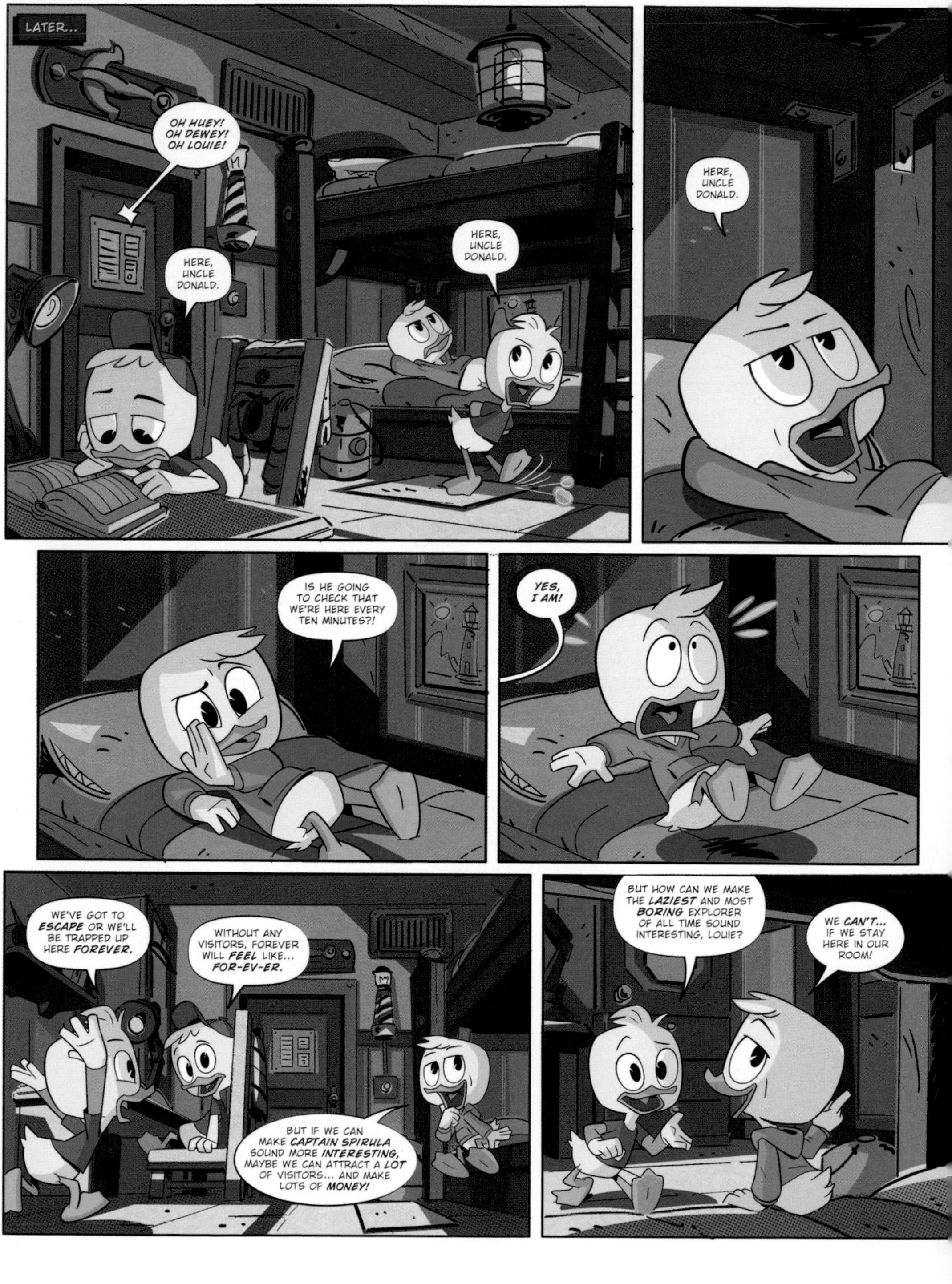
LATER...
OH HUEY! OH DEWEY! OH LOUIE!
HERE, UNCLE DONALD.
HERE, UNCLE DONALD.
HERE, UNCLE DONALD.
IS HE GOING TO CHECK THAT WE'RE HERE EVERY TEN MINUTES?!
YES, I AM!
WE'VE GOT TO ESCAPE OR WE'LL BE TRAPPED UP HERE FOREVER.
WITHOUT ANY VISITORS, FOREVER WILL FEEL LIKE... FOR-EV-ER.
BUT IF WE CAN MAKE CAPTAIN SPIRULA SOUND MORE INTERESTING, MAYBE WE CAN ATTRACT A LOT OF VISITORS... AND MAKE LOTS OF MONEY!
BUT HOW CAN WE MAKE THE LAZIEST AND MOST BORING EXPLORER OF ALL TIME SOUND INTERESTING, LOUIE?
WE CAN'T... IF WE STAY HERE IN OUR ROOM!

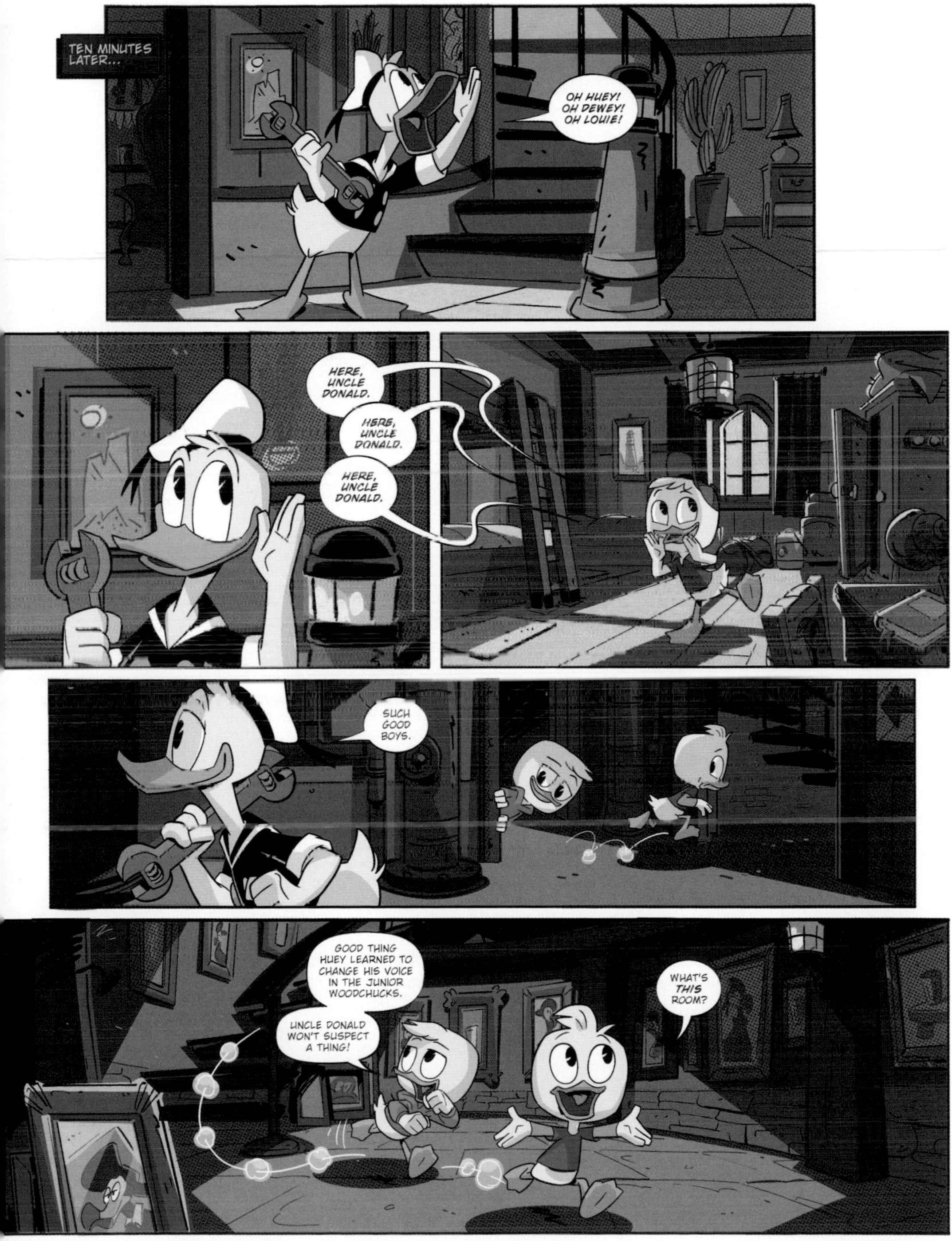
TEN MINUTES LATER...
OH HUEY! OH DEWEY! OH LOUIE!
HERE, UNCLE DONALD.
HERE, UNCLE DONALD.
HERE, UNCLE DONALD.
SUCH GOOD BOYS.
GOOD THING HUEY LEARNED TO CHANGE HIS VOICE IN THE JUNIOR WOODCHUCKS.
UNCLE DONALD WON'T SUSPECT A THING!
WHAT'S THIS ROOM?

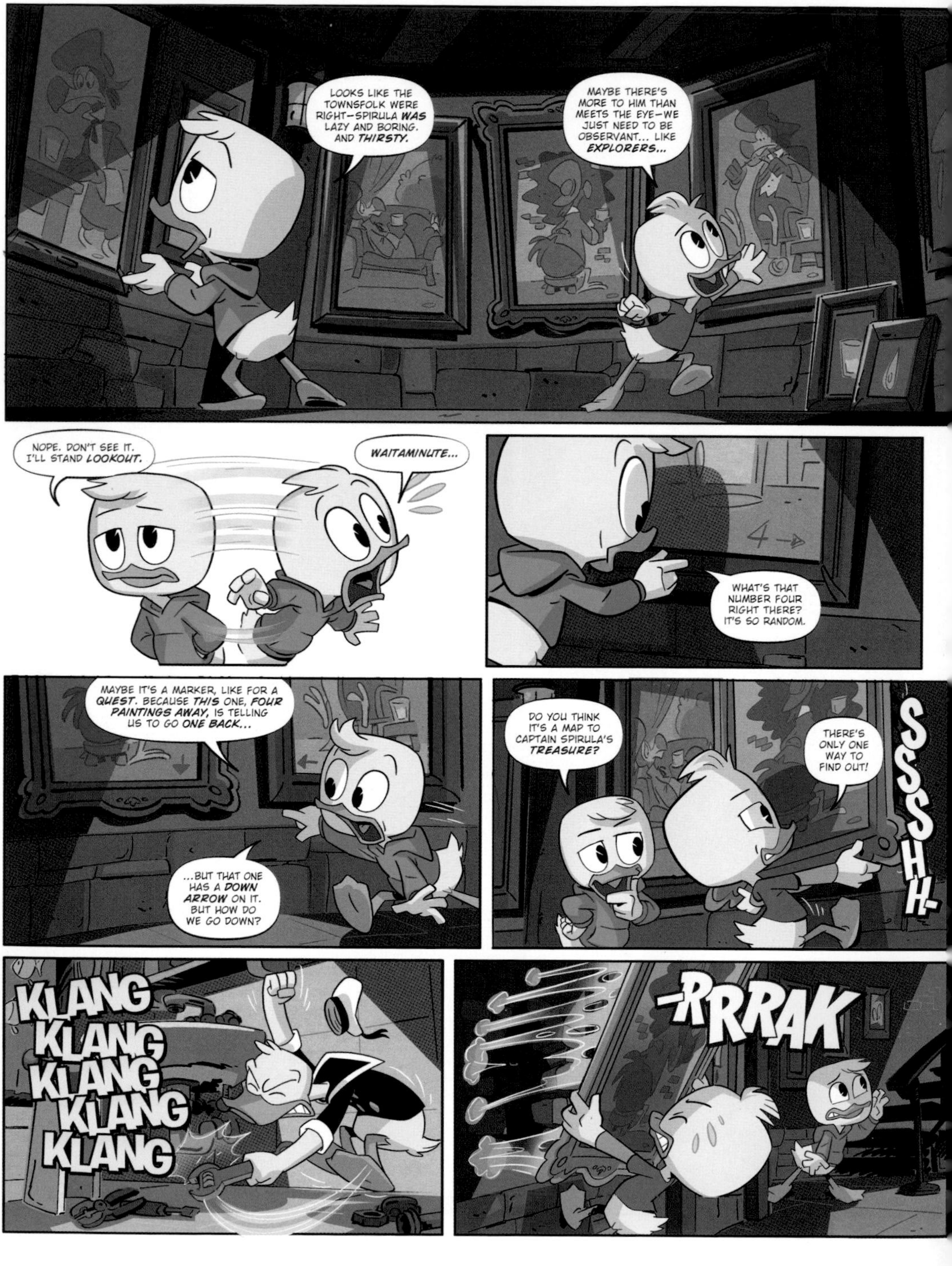

LOOKS LIKE THE TOWNSFOLK WERE RIGHT—SPIRULA WAS LAZY AND BORING. AND THIRSTY.
MAYBE THERE'S MORE TO HIM THAN MEETS THE EYE—WE JUST NEED TO BE OBSERVANT... LIKE EXPLORERS...
NOPE. DON'T SEE IT. I'LL STAND LOOKOUT.
WAITAMINUTE...
4
WHAT'S THAT NUMBER FOUR RIGHT THERE? IT'S SO RANDOM.
MAYBE IT'S A MARKER, LIKE FOR A QUEST. BECAUSE THIS ONE, FOUR PAINTINGS AWAY, IS TELLING US TO GO ONE BACK...
...BUT THAT ONE HAS A DOWN ARROW ON IT. BUT HOW DO WE GO DOWN?
DO YOU THINK IT'S A MAP TO CAPTAIN SPIRULA'S TREASURE?
THERE'S ONLY ONE WAY TO FIND OUT!
SSSHH-
KLANG KLANG KLANG KLANG KLANG
-RRRAK

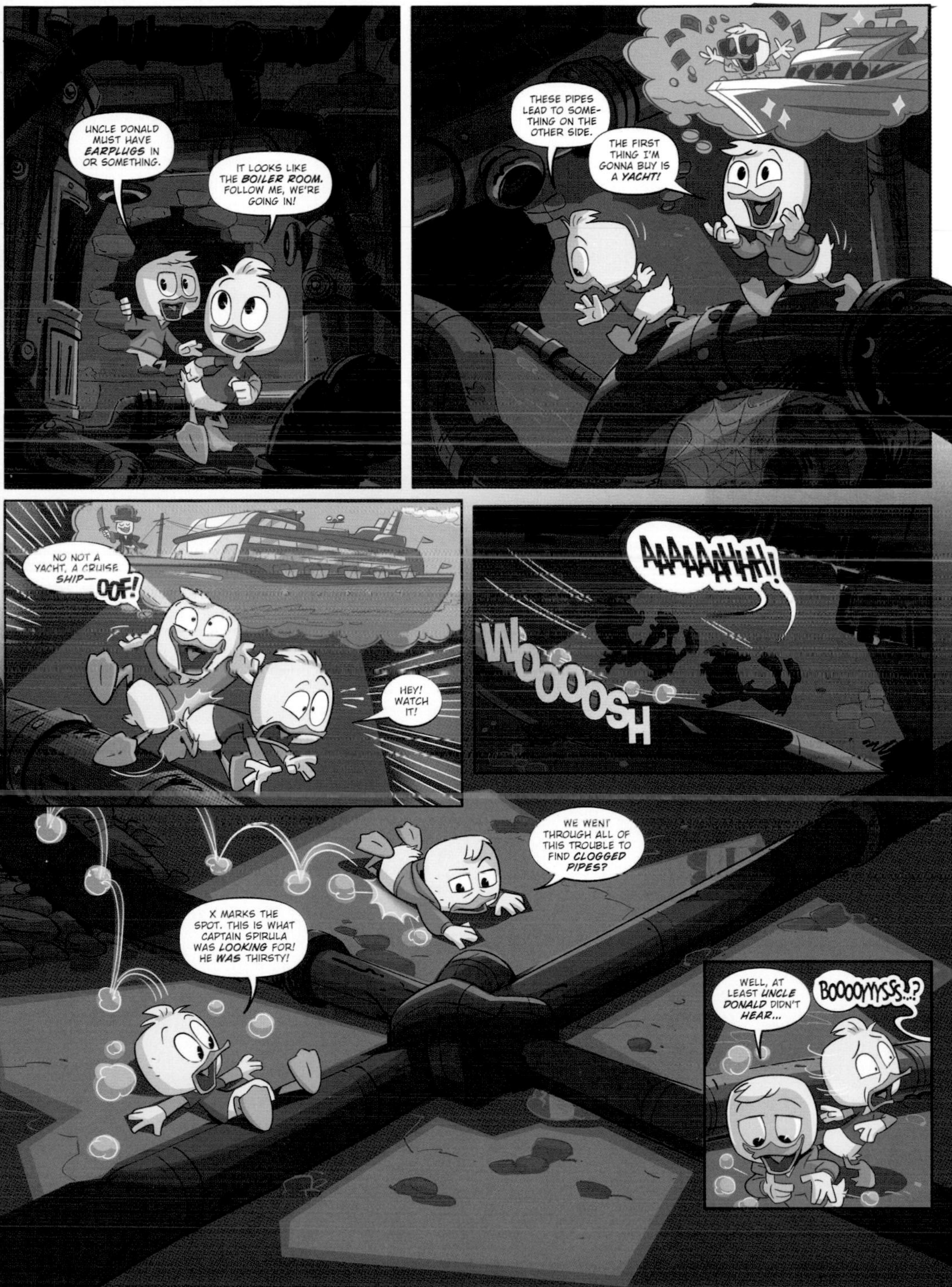
UNCLE DONALD MUST HAVE EARPLUGS IN OR SOMETHING.
IT LOOKS LIKE THE BOILER ROOM. FOLLOW ME, WE'RE GOING IN!
THESE PIPES LEAD TO SOMETHING ON THE OTHER SIDE.
THE FIRST THING I'M GONNA BUY IS A YACHT!
NO NOT A YACHT, A CRUISE SHIP—OOF!
HEY! WATCH IT!
AAAAAHHH!
WOOOOOSH
WE WENT THROUGH ALL OF THIS TROUBLE TO FIND CLOGGED PIPES?
X MARKS THE SPOT. THIS IS WHAT CAPTAIN SPIRULA WAS LOOKING FOR! HE WAS THIRSTY!
WELL, AT LEAST UNCLE DONALD DIDN'T HEAR...
BOOOOYYYSSS...?

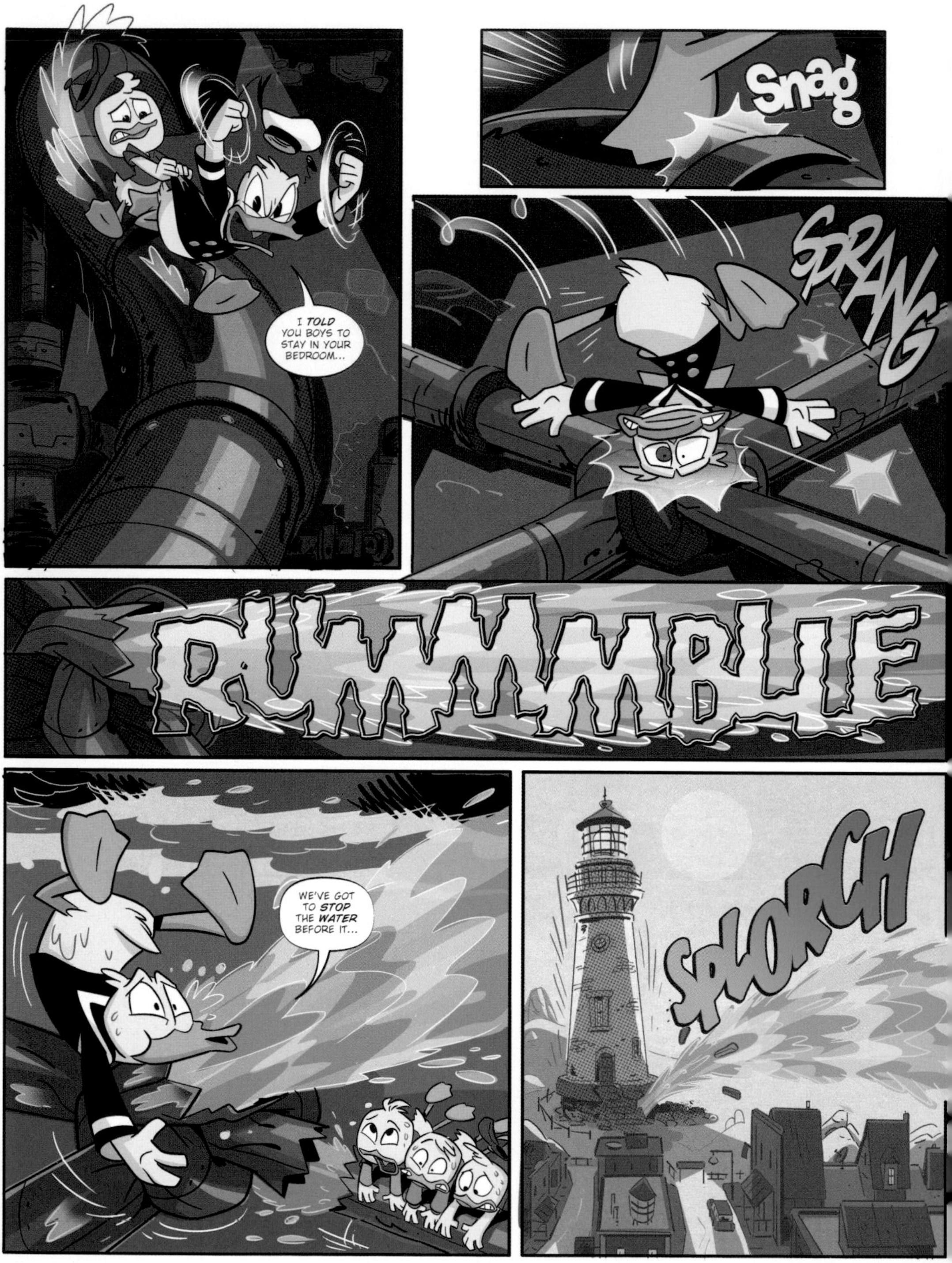
I TOLD YOU BOYS TO STAY IN YOUR BEDROOM...
Snag
SPRANG
RUMMMBLLE
WE'VE GOT TO STOP THE WATER BEFORE IT...
SPLORCH

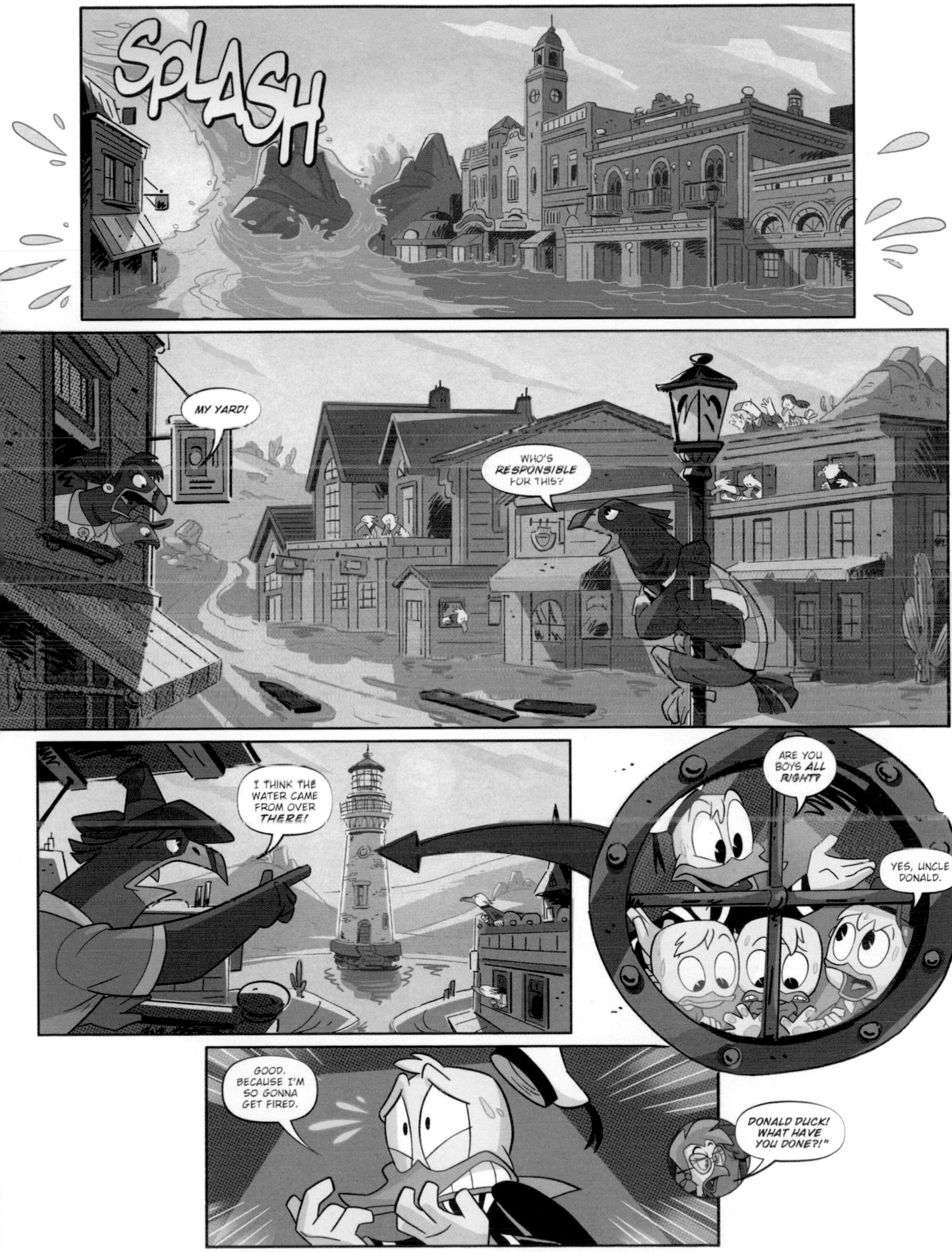
SPLASH
MY YARD!
WHO'S RESPONSIBLE FOR THIS?
I THINK THE WATER CAME FROM OVER THERE!
ARE YOU BOYS ALL RIGHT?
YES, UNCLE DONALD.
GOOD. BECAUSE I'M SO GONNA GET FIRED.
DONALD DUCK! WHAT HAVE YOU DONE?!"

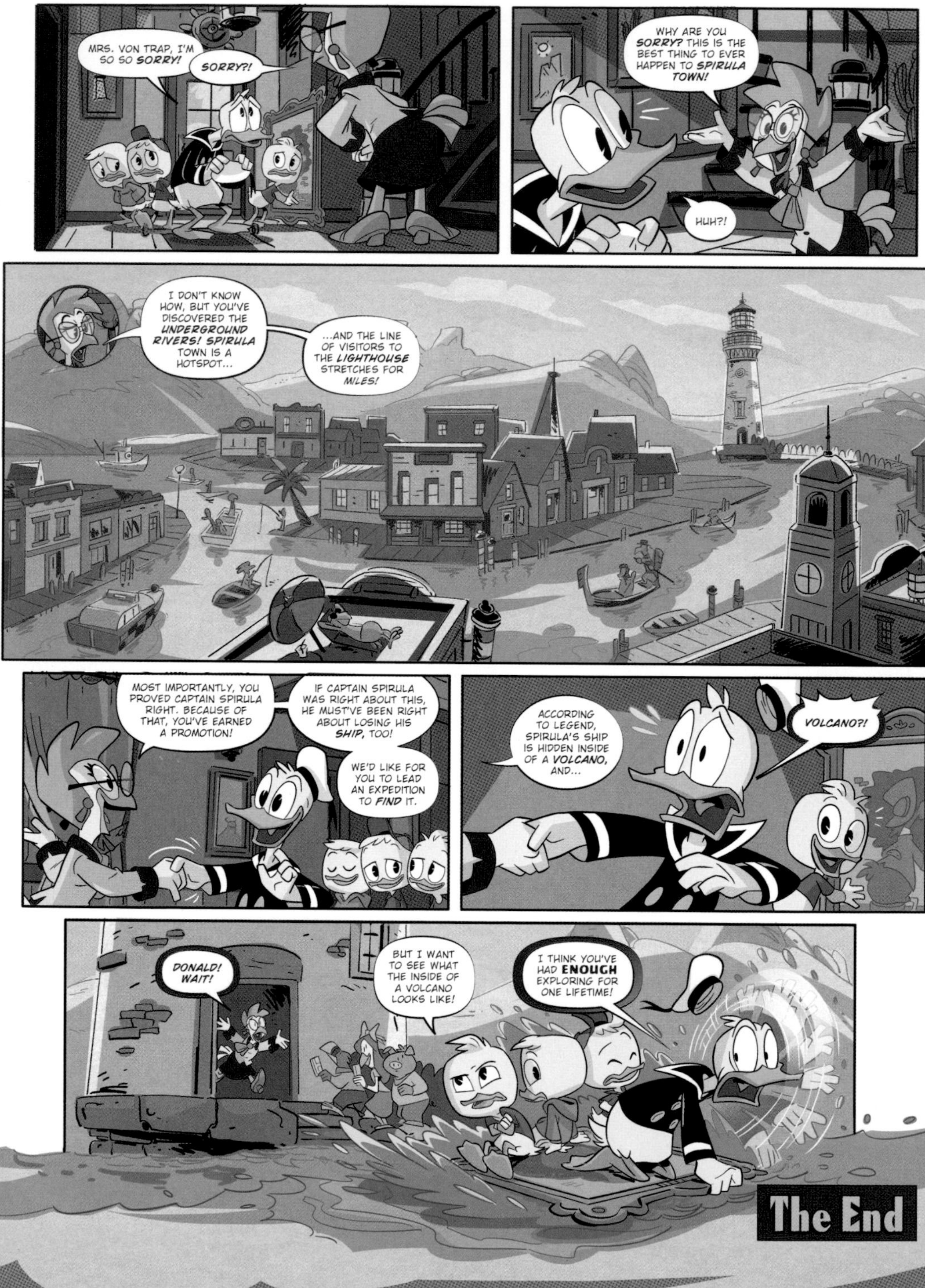
MRS. VON TRAP, I'M SO SO SORRY!
SORRY?!
WHY ARE YOU SORRY? THIS IS THE BEST THING TO EVER HAPPEN TO SPIRULA TOWN!
HUH?!
I DON'T KNOW HOW, BUT YOU'VE DISCOVERED THE UNDERGROUND RIVERS! SPIRULA TOWN IS A HOTSPOT...
...AND THE LINE OF VISITORS TO THE LIGHTHOUSE STRETCHES FOR MILES!
MOST IMPORTANTLY, YOU PROVED CAPTAIN SPIRULA RIGHT. BECAUSE OF THAT, YOU'VE EARNED A PROMOTION!
IF CAPTAIN SPIRULA WAS RIGHT ABOUT THIS, HE MUST'VE BEEN RIGHT ABOUT LOSING HIS SHIP, TOO!
WE'D LIKE FOR YOU TO LEAD AN EXPEDITION TO FIND IT.
ACCORDING TO LEGEND, SPIRULA'S SHIP IS HIDDEN INSIDE OF A VOLCANO, AND...
VOLCANO?!
DONALD! WAIT!
BUT I WANT TO SEE WHAT THE INSIDE OF A VOLCANO LOOKS LIKE!
I THINK YOU'VE HAD ENOUGH EXPLORING FOR ONE LIFETIME!
The End

Disney DuckTales

THE GREAT EXPERIMENT OF THE WASHING MACHINE!

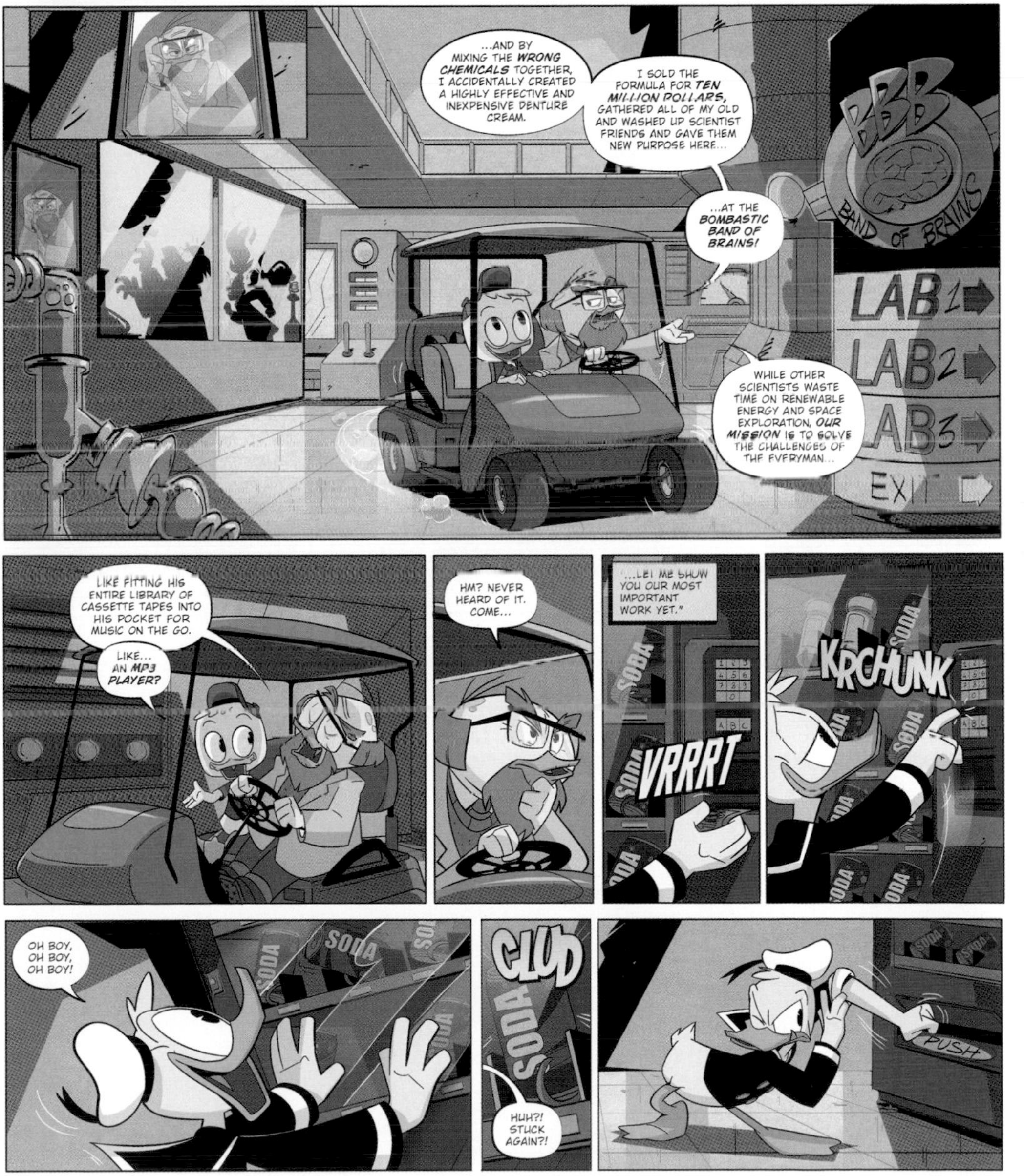
...AND BY MIXING THE WRONG CHEMICALS TOGETHER, I ACCIDENTALLY CREATED A HIGHLY EFFECTIVE AND INEXPENSIVE DENTURE CREAM.
I SOLD THE FORMULA FOR TEN MILLION DOLLARS, GATHERED ALL OF MY OLD AND WASHED UP SCIENTIST FRIENDS AND GAVE THEM NEW PURPOSE HERE...
...AT THE BOMBASTIC BAND OF BRAINS!
BBB
BAND OF BRAINS
LAB 1
LAB 2
LAB 3
EXIT
WHILE OTHER SCIENTISTS WASTE TIME ON RENEWABLE ENERGY AND SPACE EXPLORATION, OUR MISSION IS TO SOLVE THE CHALLENGES OF THE EVERYMAN...
LIKE FITTING HIS ENTIRE LIBRARY OF CASSETTE TAPES INTO HIS POCKET FOR MUSIC ON THE GO.
LIKE... AN MP3 PLAYER?
HM? NEVER HEARD OF IT. COME...
"...LET ME SHOW YOU OUR MOST IMPORTANT WORK YET."
SODA
VRRRT
KRCHUNK
OH BOY, OH BOY, OH BOY!
CLUD
HUH?! STUCK AGAIN?!
PUSH

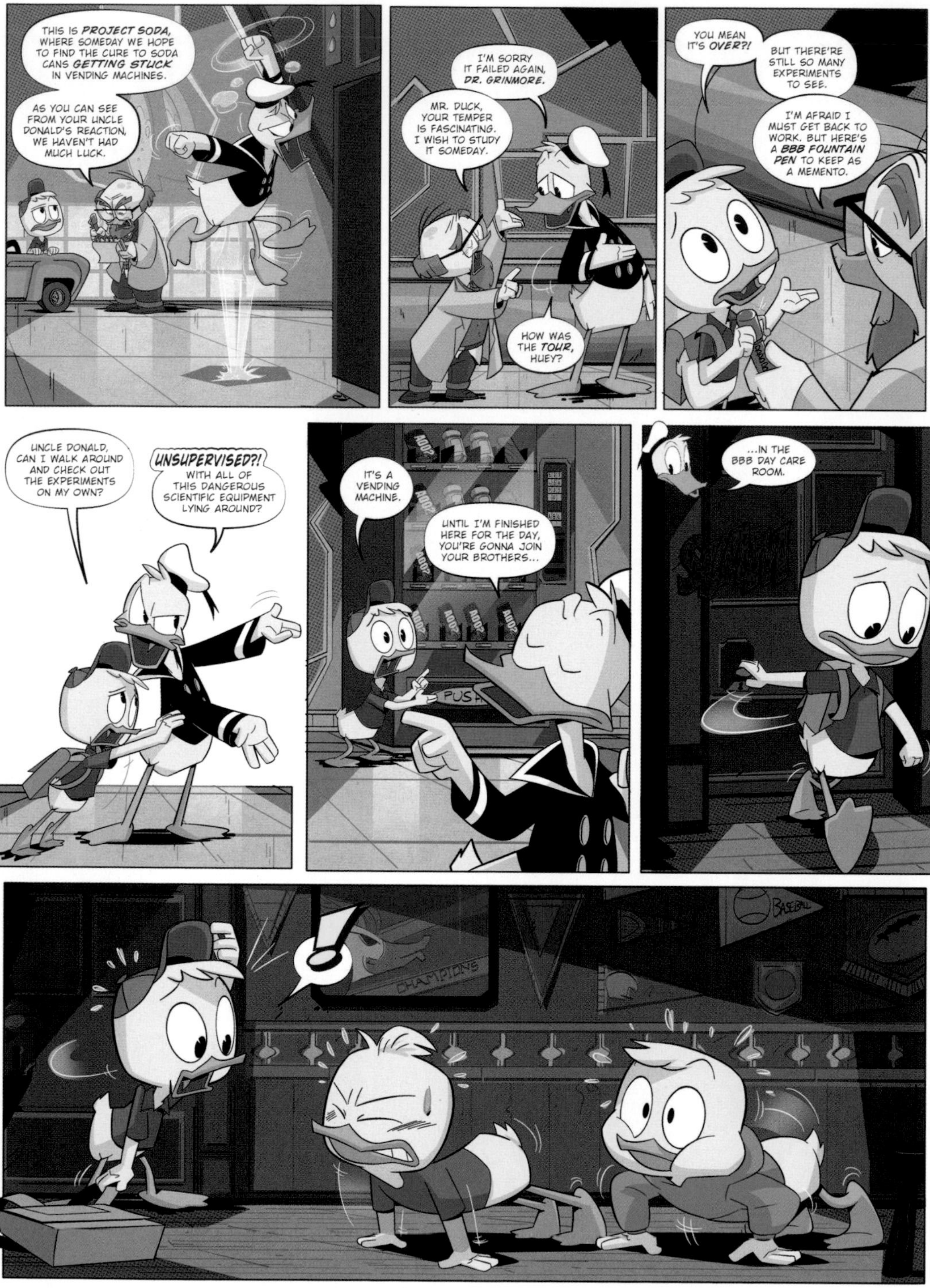

THIS IS PROJECT SODA, WHERE SOMEDAY WE HOPE TO FIND THE CURE TO SODA CANS GETTING STUCK IN VENDING MACHINES.
AS YOU CAN SEE FROM YOUR UNCLE DONALD'S REACTION, WE HAVEN'T HAD MUCH LUCK.
I'M SORRY IT FAILED AGAIN, DR. GRINMORE.
MR. DUCK, YOUR TEMPER IS FASCINATING. I WISH TO STUDY IT SOMEDAY.
HOW WAS THE TOUR, HUEY?
YOU MEAN IT'S OVER?!
BUT THERE'RE STILL SO MANY EXPERIMENTS TO SEE.
I'M AFRAID I MUST GET BACK TO WORK. BUT HERE'S A BBB FOUNTAIN PEN TO KEEP AS A MEMENTO.
UNCLE DONALD, CAN I WALK AROUND AND CHECK OUT THE EXPERIMENTS ON MY OWN?
UNSUPERVISED?! WITH ALL OF THIS DANGEROUS SCIENTIFIC EQUIPMENT LYING AROUND?
IT'S A VENDING MACHINE.
UNTIL I'M FINISHED HERE FOR THE DAY, YOU'RE GONNA JOIN YOUR BROTHERS...
...IN THE BBB DAY CARE ROOM.
CHAMPIONS
BASEBALL

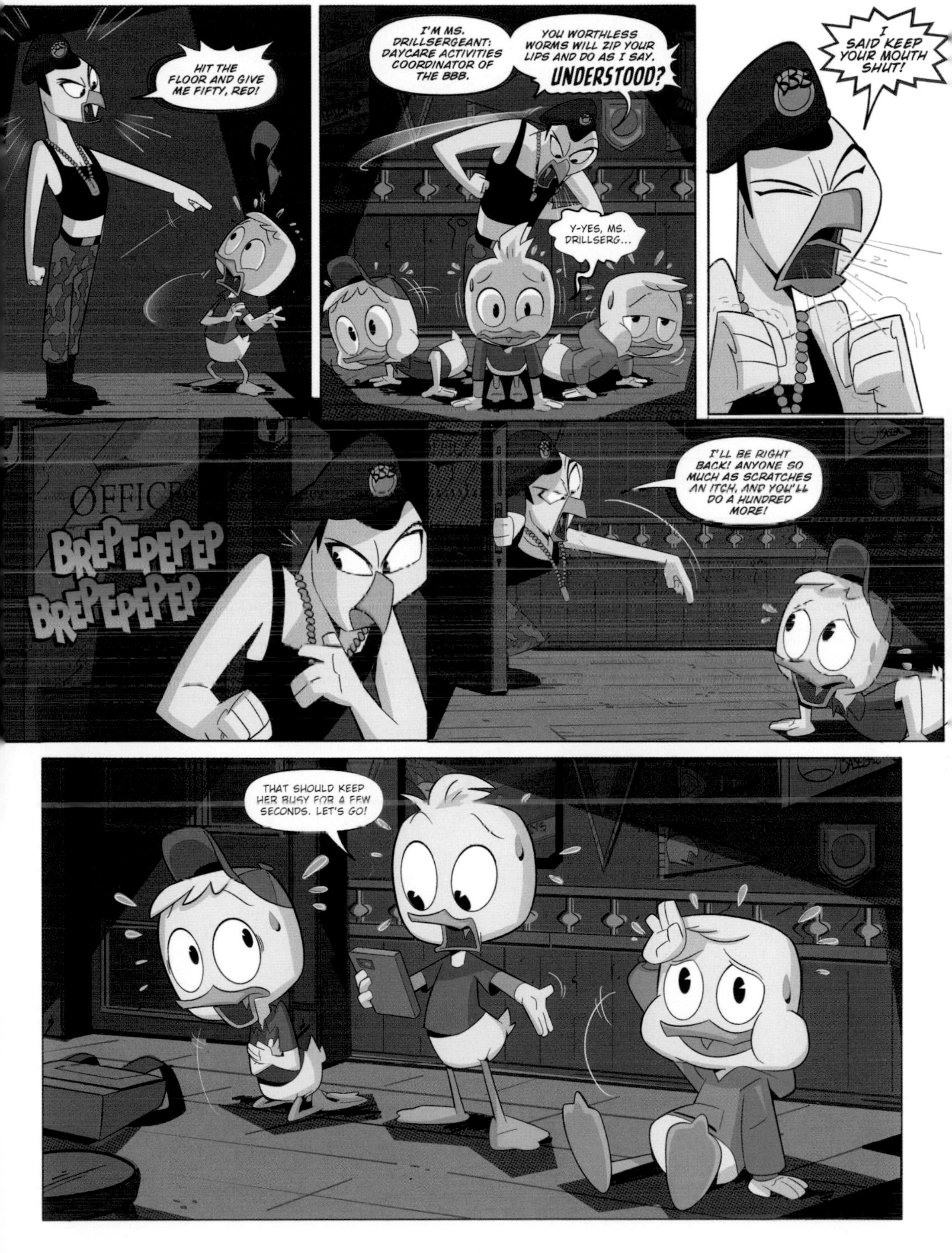
HIT THE FLOOR AND GIVE ME FIFTY, RED!
I'M MS. DRILLSERGEANT: DAYCARE ACTIVITIES COORDINATOR OF THE BBB.
YOU WORTHLESS WORMS WILL ZIP YOUR LIPS AND DO AS I SAY. UNDERSTOOD?
Y-YES, MS. DRILLSERG...
I SAID KEEP YOUR MOUTH SHUT!
OFFICE
BREPEPEPEP
BREPEPEPEP
I'LL BE RIGHT BACK! ANYONE SO MUCH AS SCRATCHES AN ITCH, AND YOU'LL DO A HUNDRED MORE!
THAT SHOULD KEEP HER BUSY FOR A FEW SECONDS. LET'S GO!

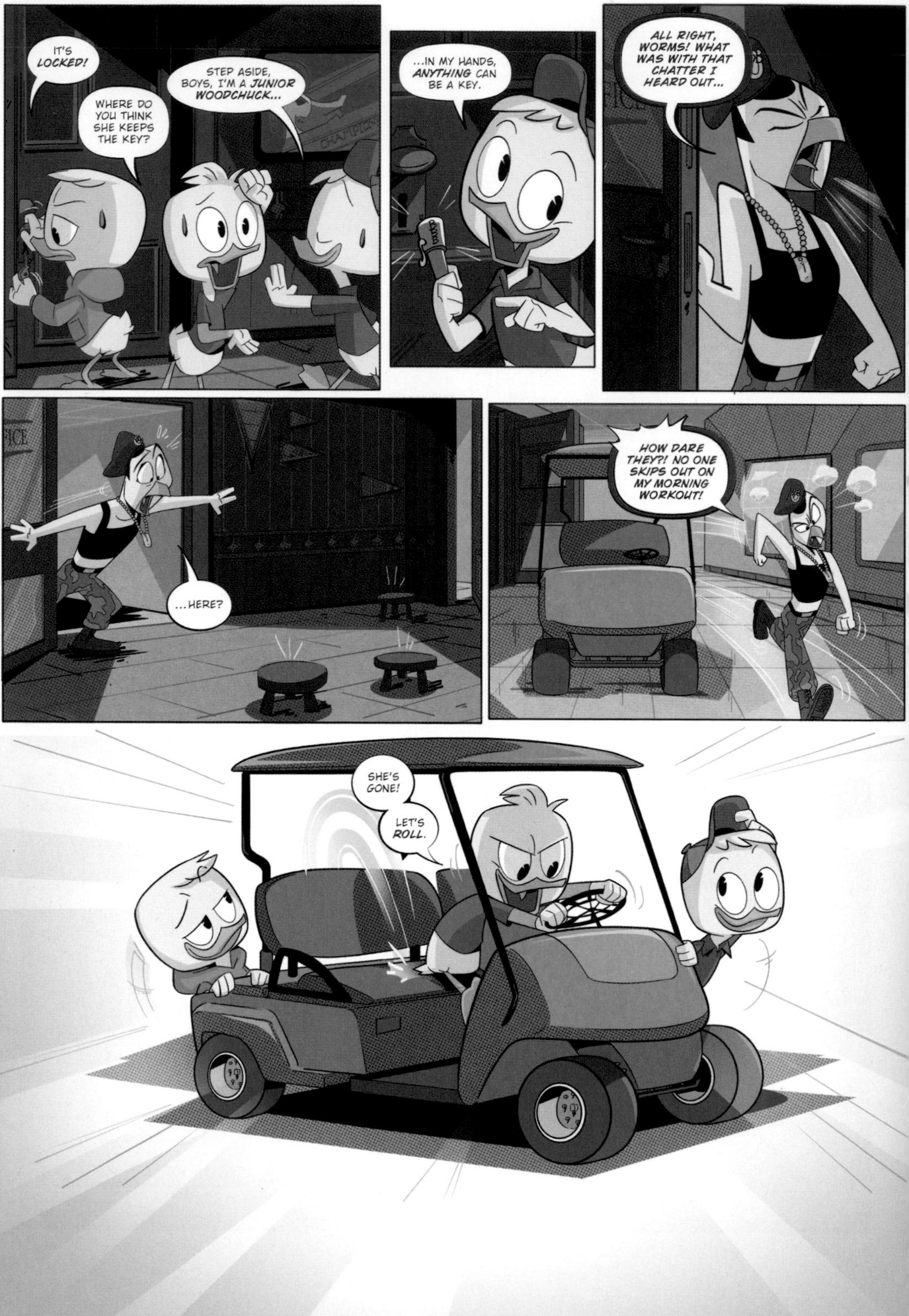
IT'S LOCKED!
WHERE DO YOU THINK SHE KEEPS THE KEY?
STEP ASIDE, BOYS, I'M A JUNIOR WOODCHUCK...
...IN MY HANDS, ANYTHING CAN BE A KEY.
ALL RIGHT, WORMS! WHAT WAS WITH THAT CHATTER I HEARD OUT...
...HERE?
HOW DARE THEY?! NO ONE SKIPS OUT ON MY MORNING WORKOUT!
SHE'S GONE!
LET'S ROLL.

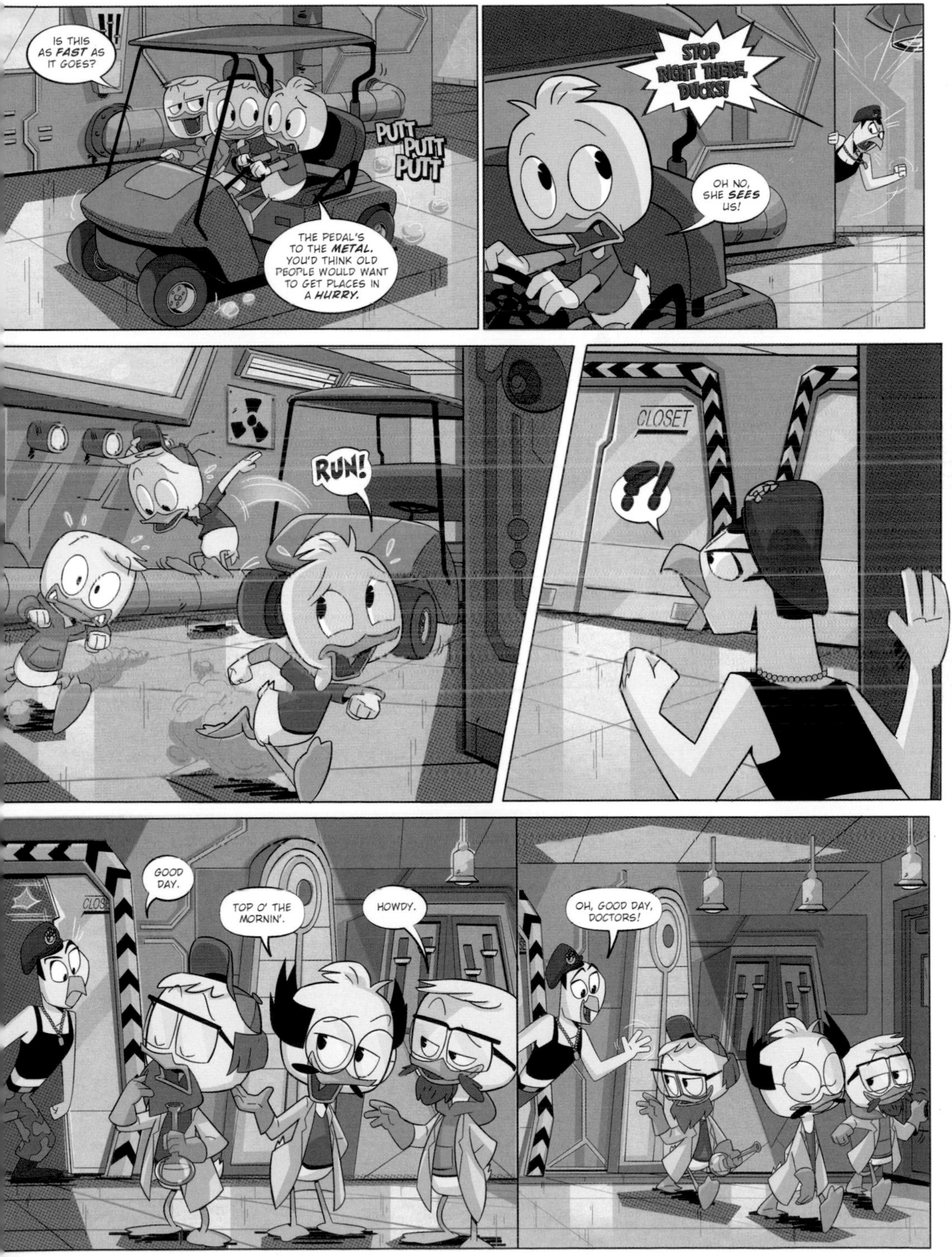
IS THIS AS FAST AS IT GOES?
PUTT PUTT PUTT
THE PEDAL'S TO THE METAL. YOU'D THINK OLD PEOPLE WOULD WANT TO GET PLACES IN A HURRY.
STOP RIGHT THERE, DUCKS!
OH NO, SHE SEES US!
RUN!
CLOSET
?!
GOOD DAY.
TOP O' THE MORNIN'.
HOWDY.
OH, GOOD DAY, DOCTORS!

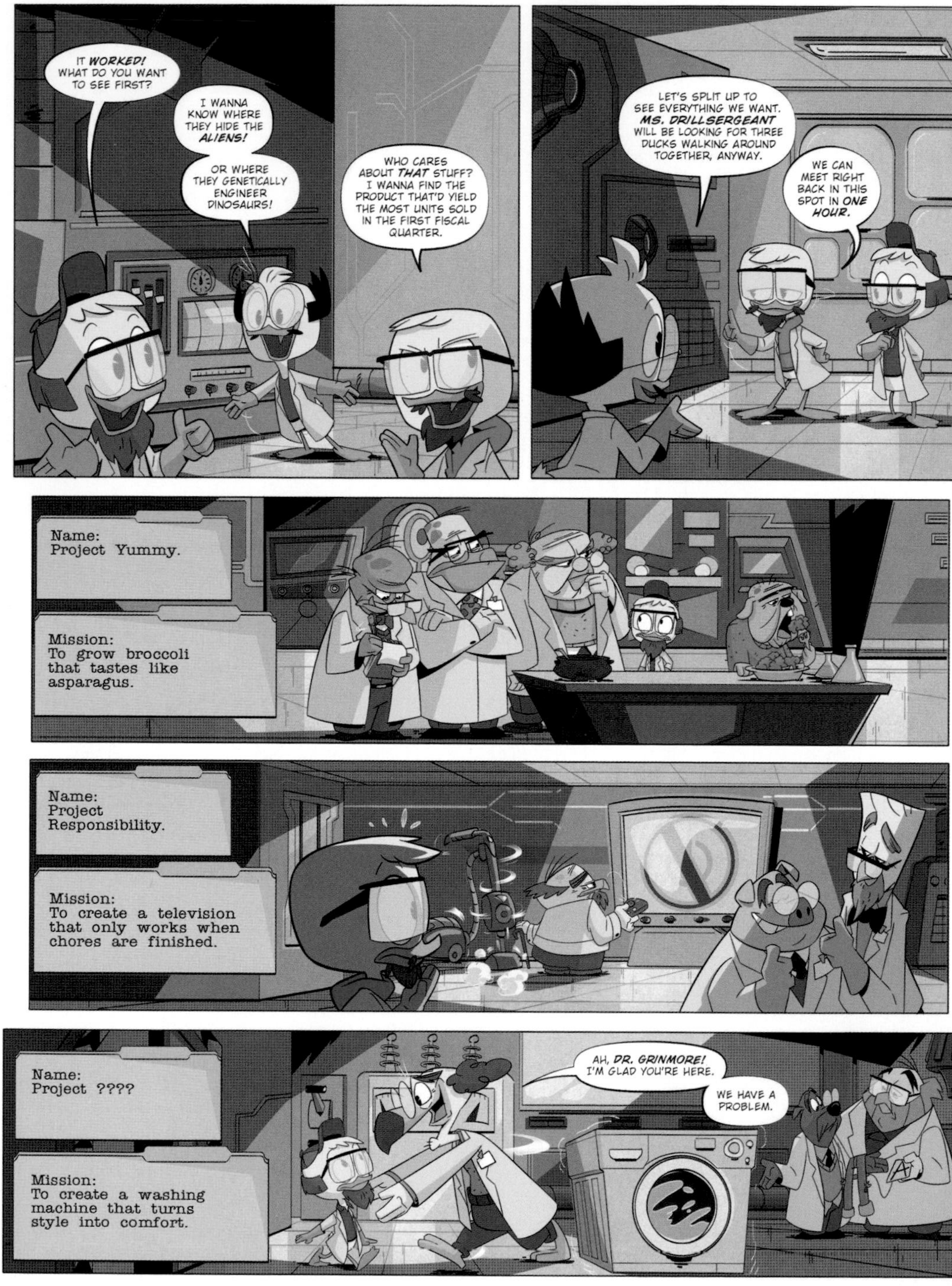

IT WORKED! WHAT DO YOU WANT TO SEE FIRST?
I WANNA KNOW WHERE THEY HIDE THE ALIENS!
OR WHERE THEY GENETICALLY ENGINEER DINOSAURS!
WHO CARES ABOUT THAT STUFF? I WANNA FIND THE PRODUCT THAT'D YIELD THE MOST UNITS SOLD IN THE FIRST FISCAL QUARTER.
LET'S SPLIT UP TO SEE EVERYTHING WE WANT. MS. DRILLSERGEANT WILL BE LOOKING FOR THREE DUCKS WALKING AROUND TOGETHER, ANYWAY.
WE CAN MEET RIGHT BACK IN THIS SPOT IN ONE HOUR.
Name: Project Yummy.
Mission: To grow broccoli that tastes like asparagus.
Name: Project Responsibility.
Mission: To create a television that only works when chores are finished.
Name: Project ????
Mission: To create a washing machine that turns style into comfort.
AH, DR. GRINMORE! I'M GLAD YOU'RE HERE.
WE HAVE A PROBLEM.

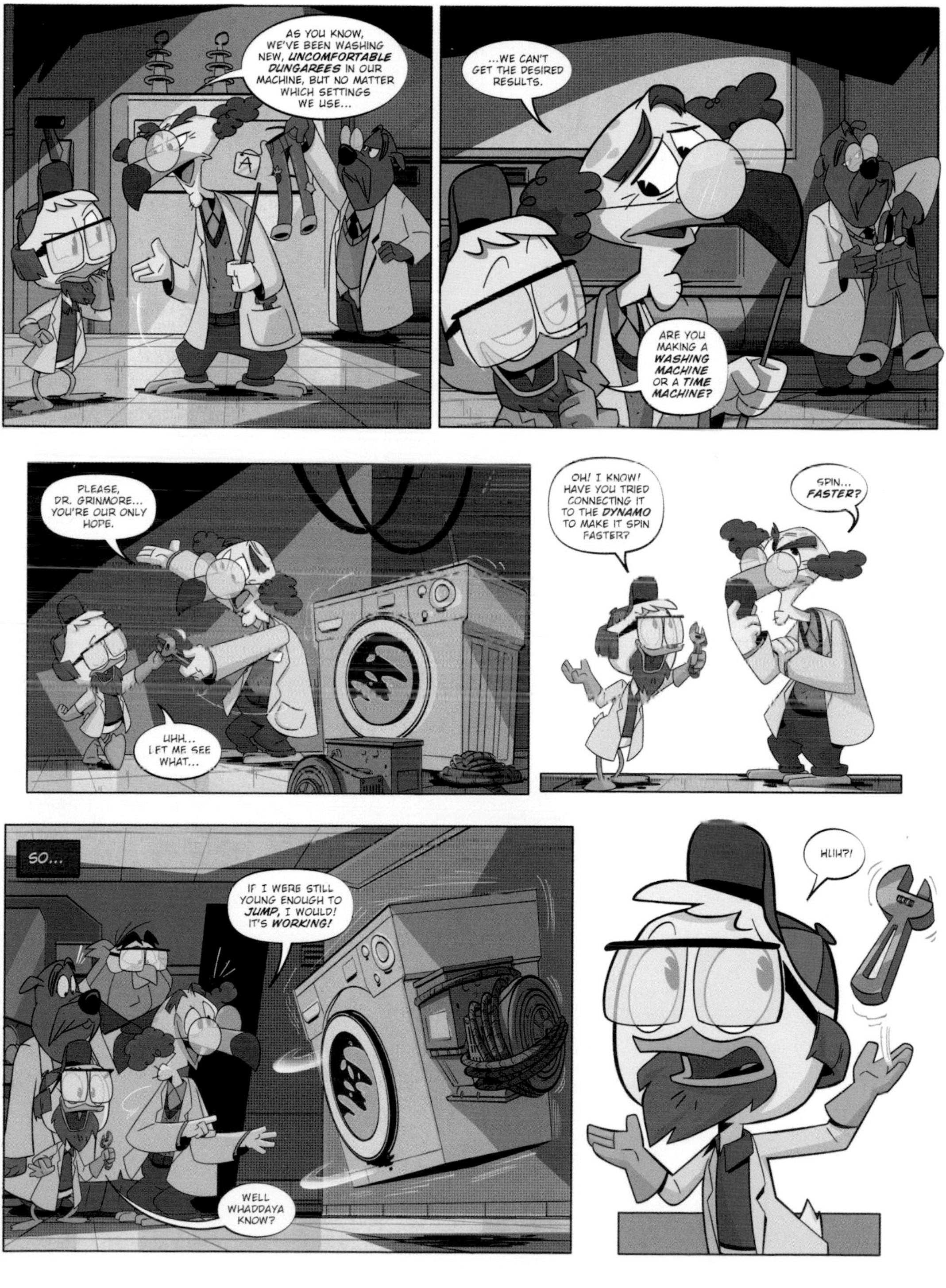
AS YOU KNOW, WE'VE BEEN WASHING NEW, UNCOMFORTABLE DUNGAREES IN OUR MACHINE, BUT NO MATTER WHICH SETTINGS WE USE...
...WE CAN'T GET THE DESIRED RESULTS.
ARE YOU MAKING A WASHING MACHINE OR A TIME MACHINE?
PLEASE, DR. GRINMORE... YOU'RE OUR ONLY HOPE.
UHH... LET ME SEE WHAT...
OH! I KNOW! HAVE YOU TRIED CONNECTING IT TO THE DYNAMO TO MAKE IT SPIN FASTER?
SPIN... FASTER?
SO...
IF I WERE STILL YOUNG ENOUGH TO JUMP, I WOULD! IT'S WORKING!
WELL WHADDAYA KNOW?
HUH?!

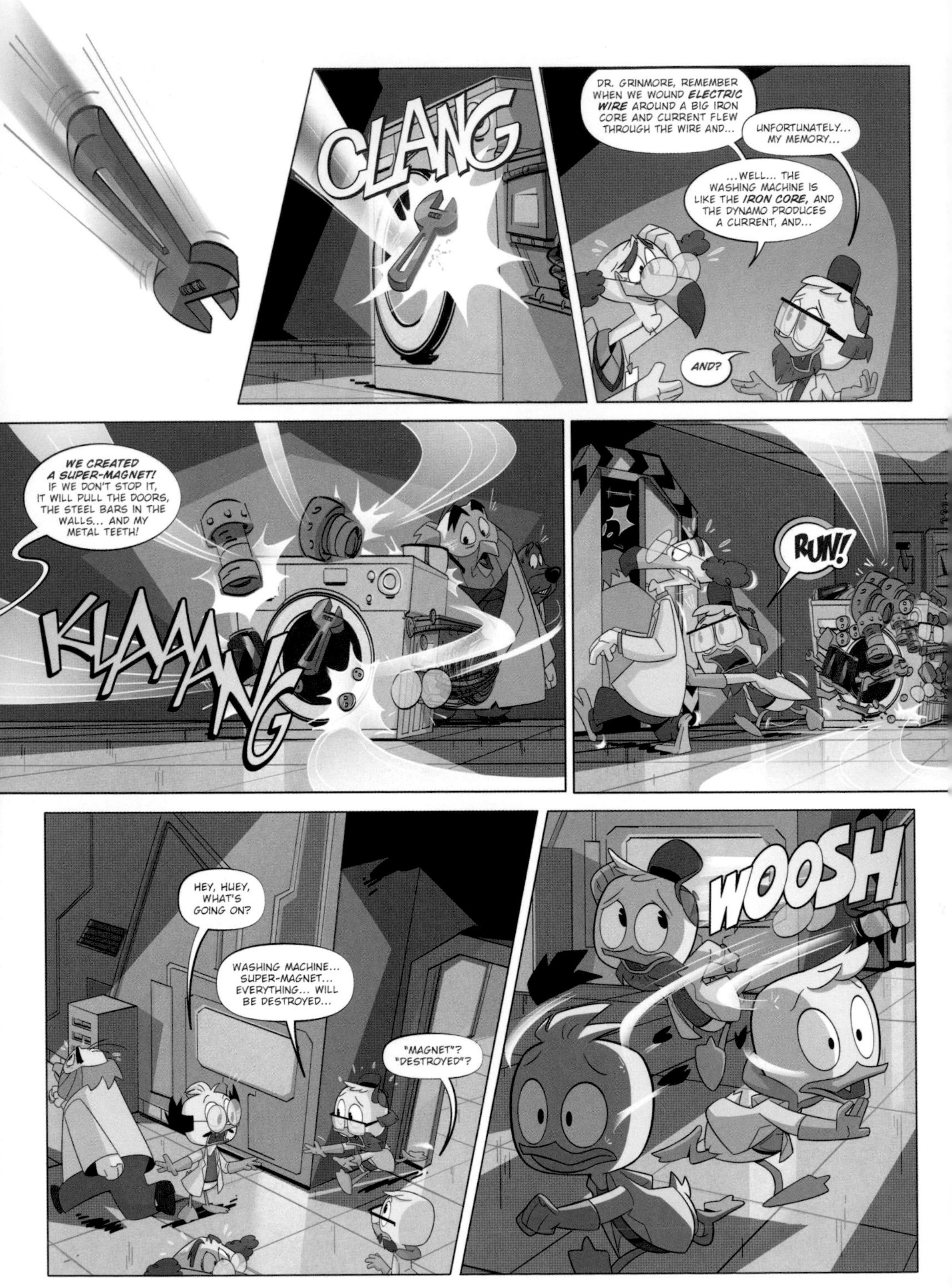
CLANG
DR. GRINMORE, REMEMBER WHEN WE WOUND ELECTRIC WIRE AROUND A BIG IRON CORE AND CURRENT FLEW THROUGH THE WIRE AND...
UNFORTUNATELY... MY MEMORY...
...WELL... THE WASHING MACHINE IS LIKE THE IRON CORE, AND THE DYNAMO PRODUCES A CURRENT, AND...
AND?
WE CREATED A SUPER-MAGNET! IF WE DON'T STOP IT, IT WILL PULL THE DOORS, THE STEEL BARS IN THE WALLS... AND MY METAL TEETH!
KLAAAANG
RUN!
HEY, HUEY, WHAT'S GOING ON?
WASHING MACHINE... SUPER-MAGNET... EVERYTHING... WILL BE DESTROYED...
"MAGNET"? "DESTROYED"?
WOOSH

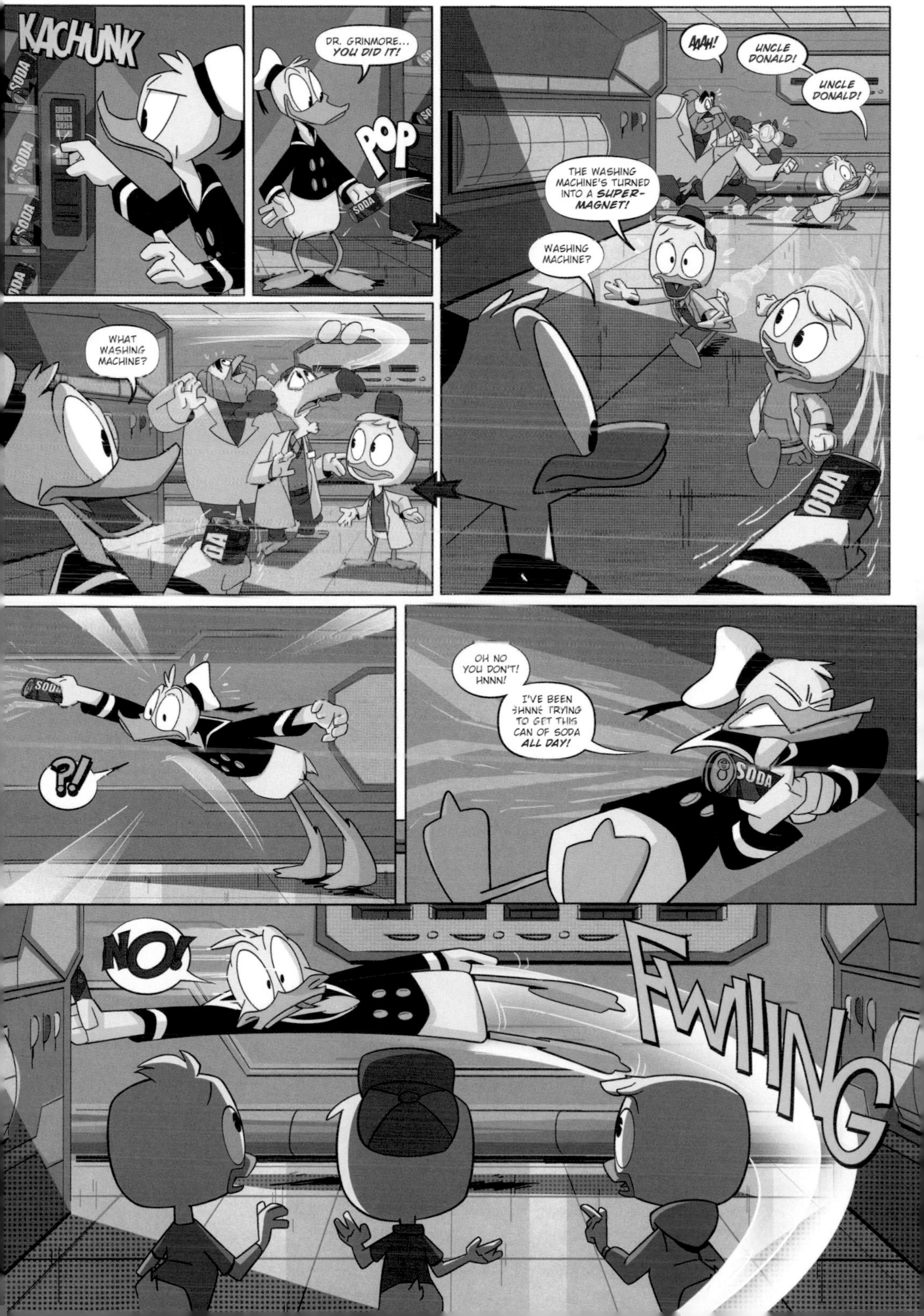
KACHUNK
SODA
DR. GRINMORE... YOU DID IT!
POP
AAAH!
UNCLE DONALD!
UNCLE DONALD!
THE WASHING MACHINE'S TURNED INTO A SUPER-MAGNET!
WASHING MACHINE?
WHAT WASHING MACHINE?
?!
OH NO YOU DON'T! HNNN!
I'VE BEEN HNNG TRYING TO GET THIS CAN OF SODA ALL DAY!
NO!
FWIING

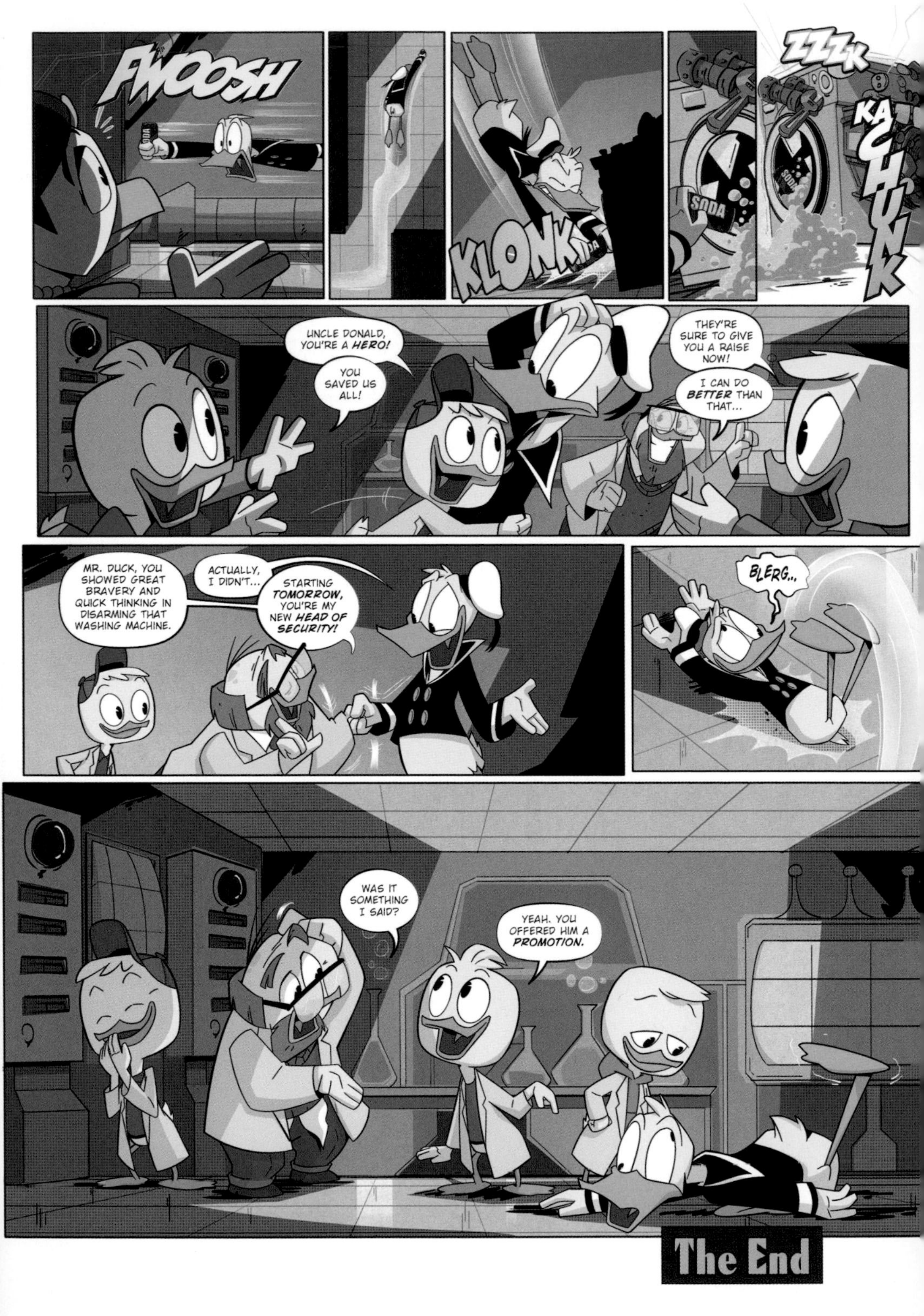
FWOOSH
KLONK
SODA
ZZZK
SODA
SODA
KA CHUNK
UNCLE DONALD, YOU'RE A HERO!
YOU SAVED US ALL!
THEY'RE SURE TO GIVE YOU A RAISE NOW!
I CAN DO BETTER THAN THAT...
MR. DUCK, YOU SHOWED GREAT BRAVERY AND QUICK THINKING IN DISARMING THAT WASHING MACHINE.
ACTUALLY, I DIDN'T...
STARTING TOMORROW, YOU'RE MY NEW HEAD OF SECURITY!
BLERG...
WAS IT SOMETHING I SAID?
YEAH. YOU OFFERED HIM A PROMOTION.
The End

Disney DuckTales

AWESOME EXPLOITS and QUESTS for rare and wonderful artifacts culled from foreboding terrain and forbidden lands! These are our journeys, these are: The Daring Adventures of Scrooge, Donald and Della Duck!

OLD MONTEPLUMAGE HAD A CHICKEN!

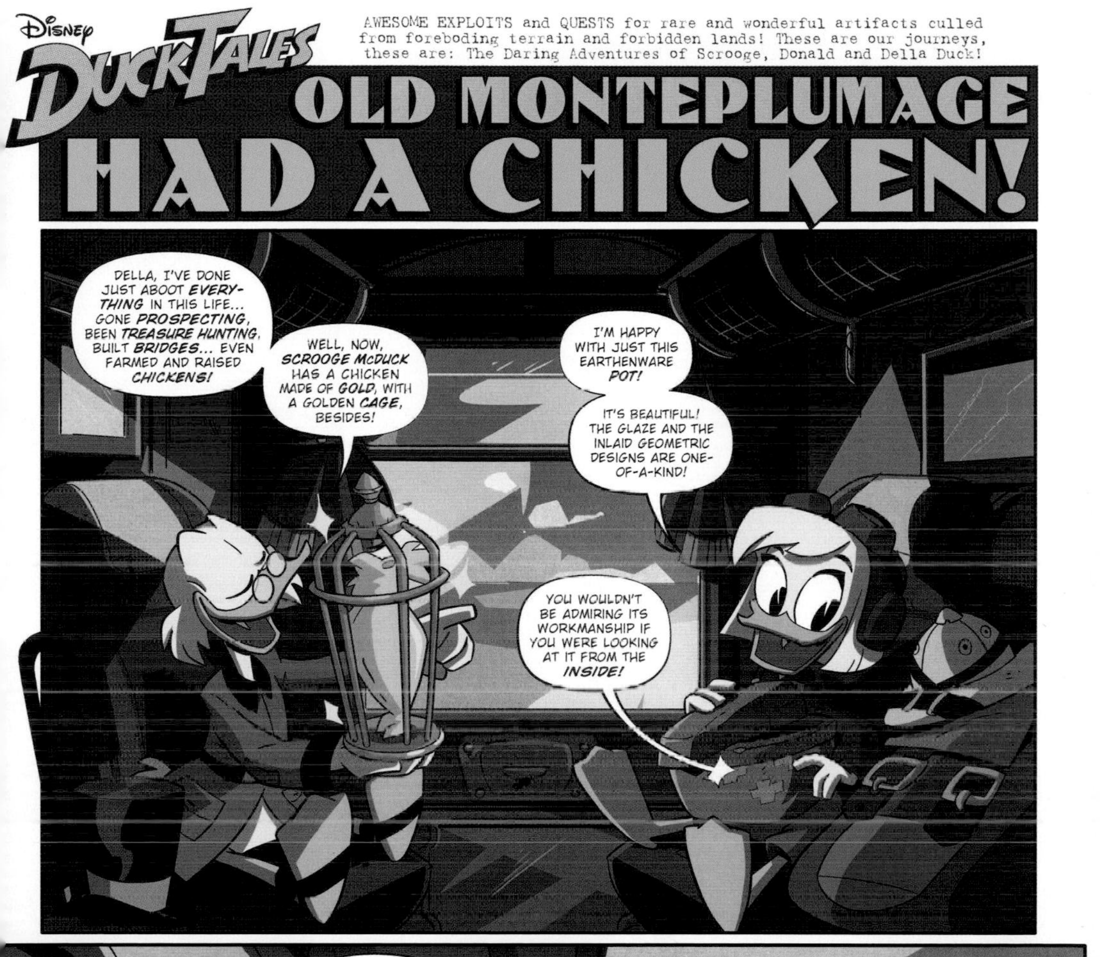
DELLA, I'VE DONE JUST ABOOT ***EVERYTHING*** IN THIS LIFE... GONE ***PROSPECTING***, BEEN ***TREASURE HUNTING***, BUILT ***BRIDGES***... EVEN FARMED AND RAISED ***CHICKENS!***
WELL, NOW, ***SCROOGE McDUCK*** HAS A CHICKEN MADE OF ***GOLD***, WITH A GOLDEN ***CAGE***, BESIDES!
I'M HAPPY WITH JUST THIS EARTHENWARE ***POT!***
IT'S BEAUTIFUL! THE GLAZE AND THE INLAID GEOMETRIC DESIGNS ARE ONE-OF-A-KIND!
YOU WOULDN'T BE ADMIRING ITS WORKMANSHIP IF YOU WERE LOOKING AT IT FROM THE ***INSIDE!***

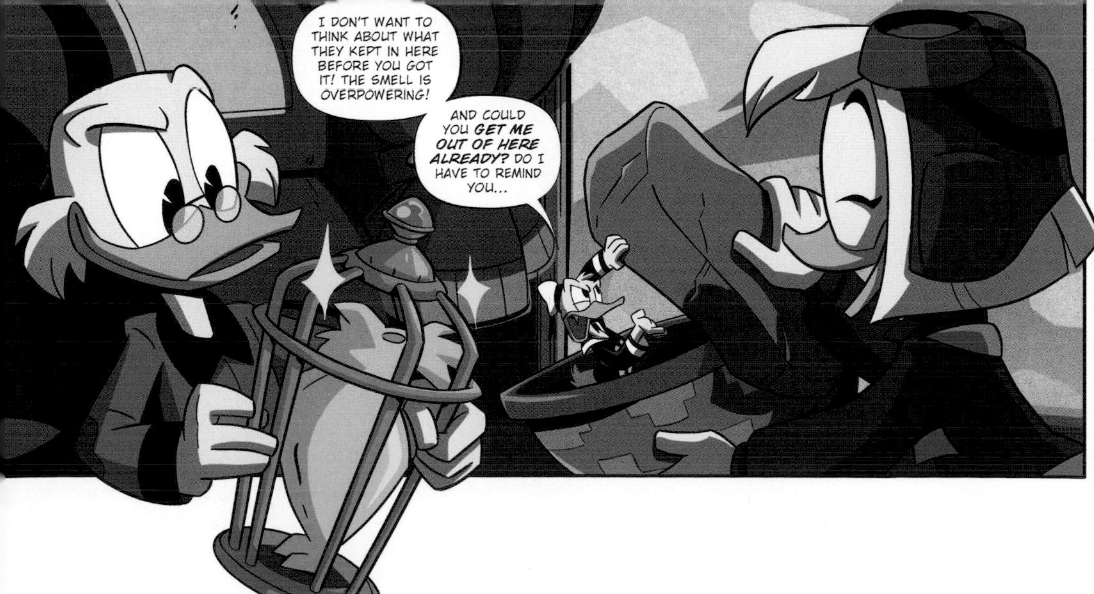
I DON'T WANT TO THINK ABOUT WHAT THEY KEPT IN HERE BEFORE YOU GOT IT! THE SMELL IS OVERPOWERING!
AND COULD YOU ***GET ME OUT OF HERE ALREADY?*** DO I HAVE TO REMIND YOU...

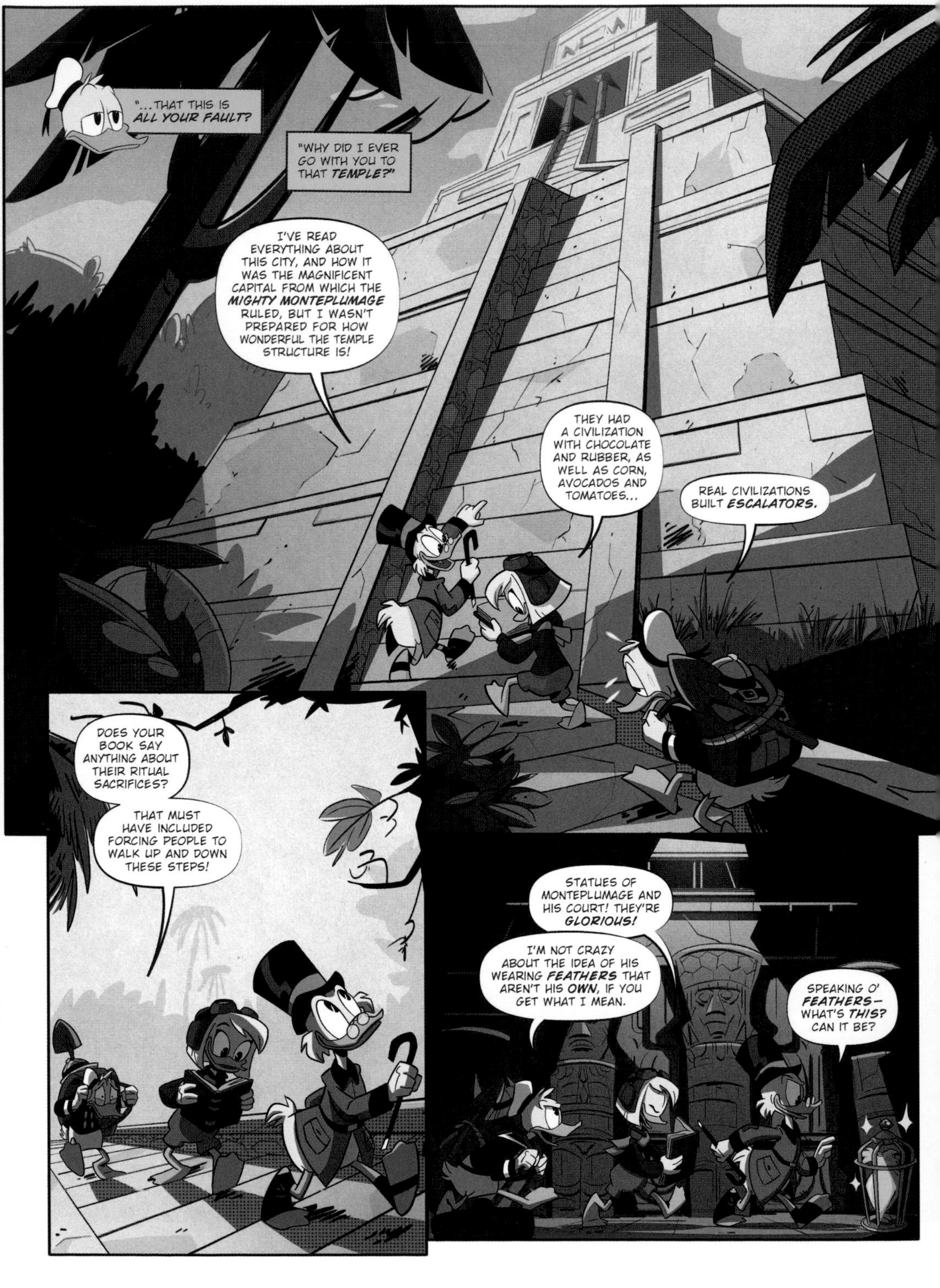
"...THAT THIS IS ALL YOUR FAULT?
"WHY DID I EVER GO WITH YOU TO THAT TEMPLE?"
I'VE READ EVERYTHING ABOUT THIS CITY, AND HOW IT WAS THE MAGNIFICENT CAPITAL FROM WHICH THE MIGHTY MONTEPLUMAGE RULED, BUT I WASN'T PREPARED FOR HOW WONDERFUL THE TEMPLE STRUCTURE IS!
THEY HAD A CIVILIZATION WITH CHOCOLATE AND RUBBER, AS WELL AS CORN, AVOCADOS AND TOMATOES...
REAL CIVILIZATIONS BUILT ESCALATORS.
DOES YOUR BOOK SAY ANYTHING ABOUT THEIR RITUAL SACRIFICES?
THAT MUST HAVE INCLUDED FORCING PEOPLE TO WALK UP AND DOWN THESE STEPS!
STATUES OF MONTEPLUMAGE AND HIS COURT! THEY'RE GLORIOUS!
I'M NOT CRAZY ABOUT THE IDEA OF HIS WEARING FEATHERS THAT AREN'T HIS OWN, IF YOU GET WHAT I MEAN.
SPEAKING O' FEATHERS— WHAT'S THIS? CAN IT BE?

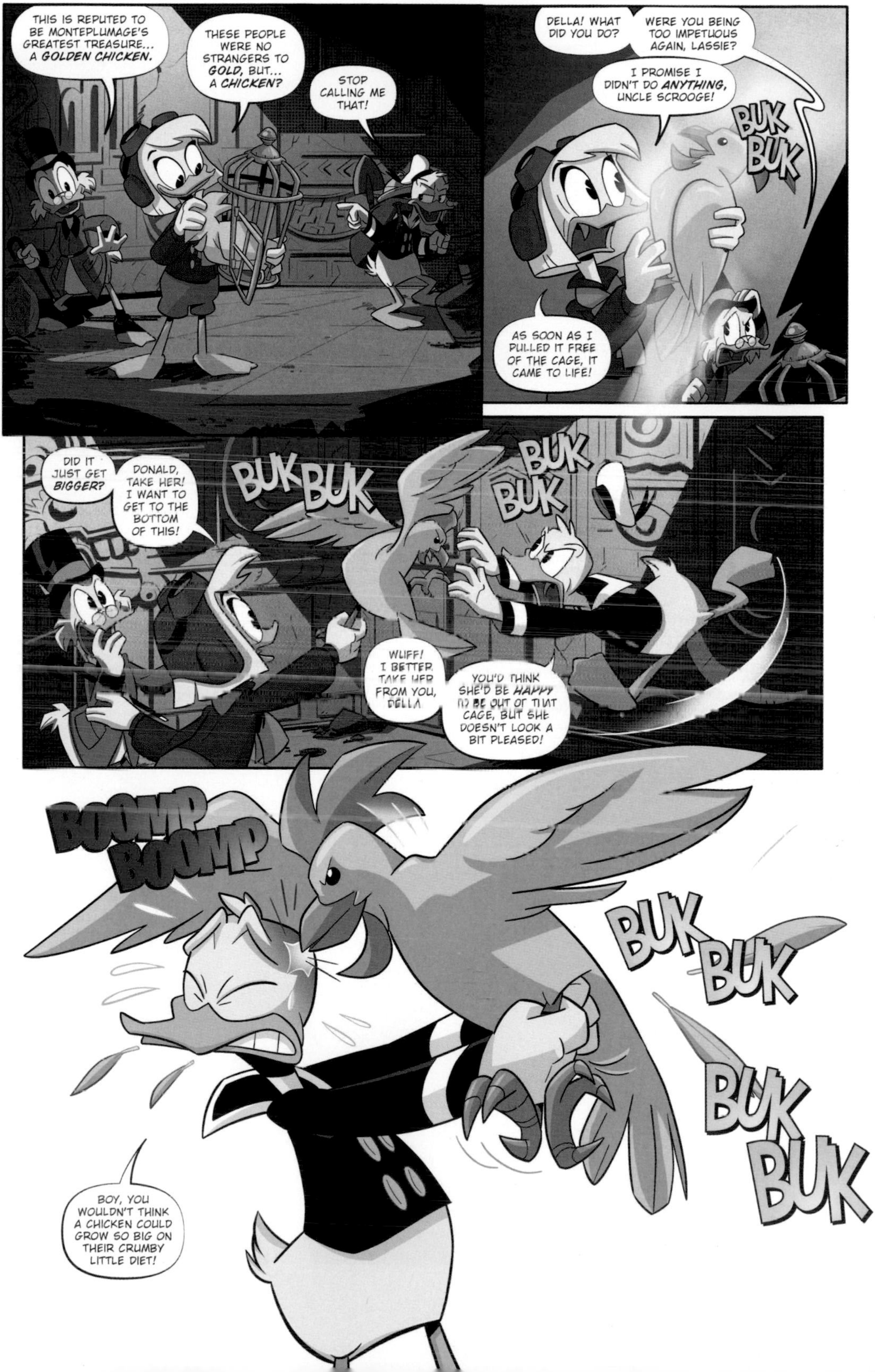
THIS IS REPUTED TO BE MONTEPLUMAGE'S GREATEST TREASURE... A GOLDEN CHICKEN.
THESE PEOPLE WERE NO STRANGERS TO GOLD, BUT... A CHICKEN?
STOP CALLING ME THAT!
DELLA! WHAT DID YOU DO?
WERE YOU BEING TOO IMPETUOUS AGAIN, LASSIE?
I PROMISE I DIDN'T DO ANYTHING, UNCLE SCROOGE!
BUK BUK
AS SOON AS I PULLED IT FREE OF THE CAGE, IT CAME TO LIFE!
DID IT JUST GET BIGGER?
DONALD, TAKE HER! I WANT TO GET TO THE BOTTOM OF THIS!
BUK BUK
BUK BUK
WUFF! I BETTER TAKE HER FROM YOU, DELLA
YOU'D THINK SHE'D BE HAPPY TO BE OUT OF THAT CAGE, BUT SHE DOESN'T LOOK A BIT PLEASED!
BOOMP BOOMP
BUK BUK
BUK BUK
BOY, YOU WOULDN'T THINK A CHICKEN COULD GROW SO BIG ON THEIR CRUMBY LITTLE DIET!

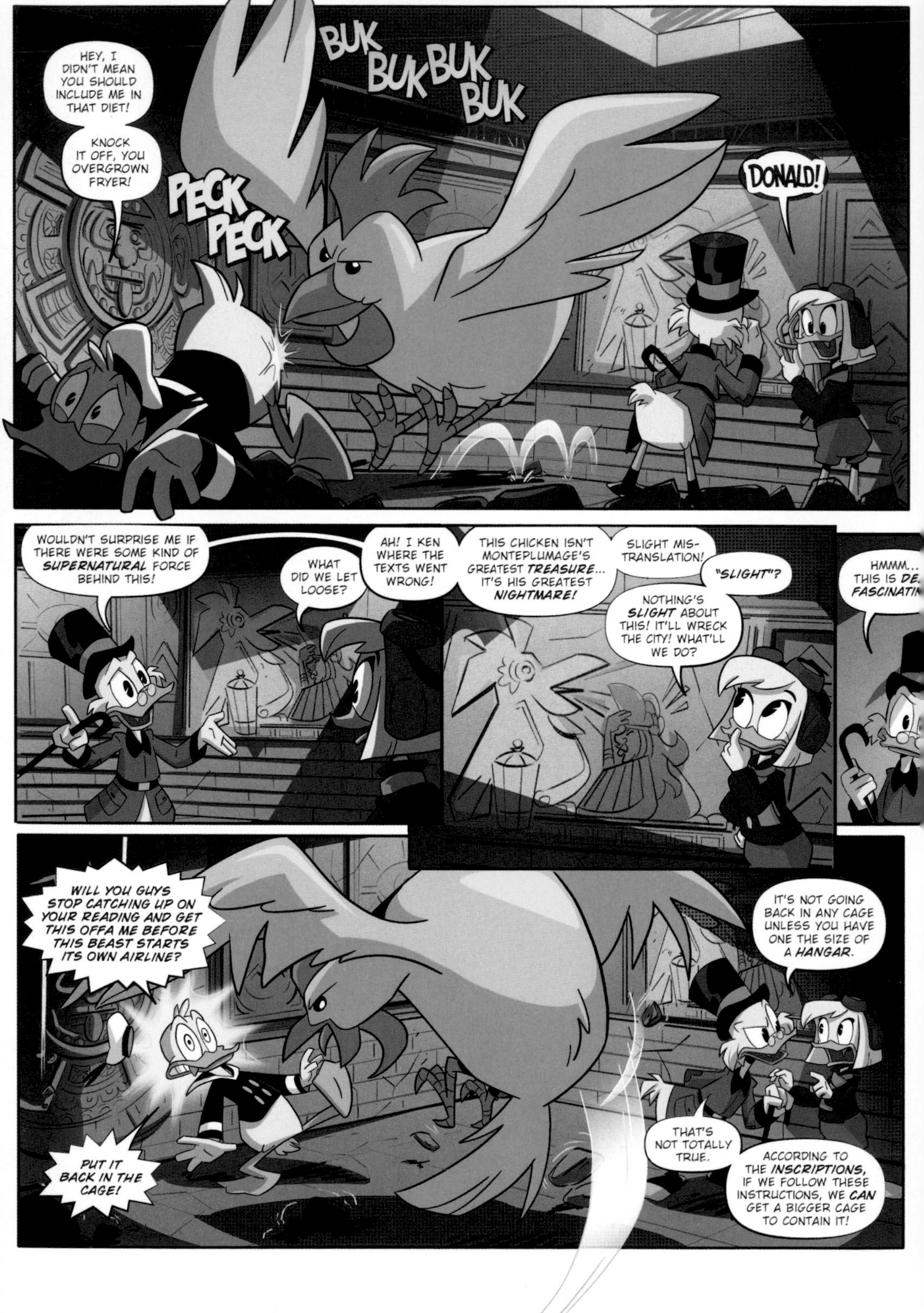
HEY, I DIDN'T MEAN YOU SHOULD INCLUDE ME IN THAT DIET!
KNOCK IT OFF, YOU OVERGROWN FRYER!
PECK PECK
BUK BUK BUK BUK
DONALD!
WOULDN'T SURPRISE ME IF THERE WERE SOME KIND OF SUPERNATURAL FORCE BEHIND THIS!
WHAT DID WE LET LOOSE?
AH! I KEN WHERE THE TEXTS WENT WRONG!
THIS CHICKEN ISN'T MONTEPLUMAGE'S GREATEST TREASURE... IT'S HIS GREATEST NIGHTMARE!
SLIGHT MIS-TRANSLATION!
"SLIGHT"?
NOTHING'S SLIGHT ABOUT THIS! IT'LL WRECK THE CITY! WHAT'LL WE DO?
WILL YOU GUYS STOP CATCHING UP ON YOUR READING AND GET THIS OFFA ME BEFORE THIS BEAST STARTS ITS OWN AIRLINE?
PUT IT BACK IN THE CAGE!
IT'S NOT GOING BACK IN ANY CAGE UNLESS YOU HAVE ONE THE SIZE OF A HANGAR.
THAT'S NOT TOTALLY TRUE.
ACCORDING TO THE INSCRIPTIONS, IF WE FOLLOW THESE INSTRUCTIONS, WE CAN GET A BIGGER CAGE TO CONTAIN IT!

THE SITUATION IS GROWING *SERIOUS!*

WHEN DOES IT EVER GROW *FRIVOLOUS?*

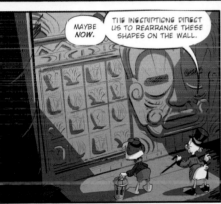

MAYBE *NOW.*

THE INSCRIPTIONS DIRECT US TO REARRANGE THESE SHAPES ON THE WALL.

WHEN WE MANAGE TO GET THREE O' THE SAME COLOR, WE'LL BE REWARDED WITH A MUCH BIGGER CAGE! AND *SOON,* I HOPE!

STAND BACK AND WATCH ME! I'VE PLAYED PLENTY OF *THOSE* GAMES BEFORE!

BUK BUK BUK BUK

THAAAAT'S NOT A GOOD SIGN!

BUT THERE'S NOTHING I CAN DO ABOUT IT! FROM HER PERSPECTIVE, I LOOK LIKE AN *EGG,* AND SHE'S NOT BUDGING OFF ME!

RRRUMBLE

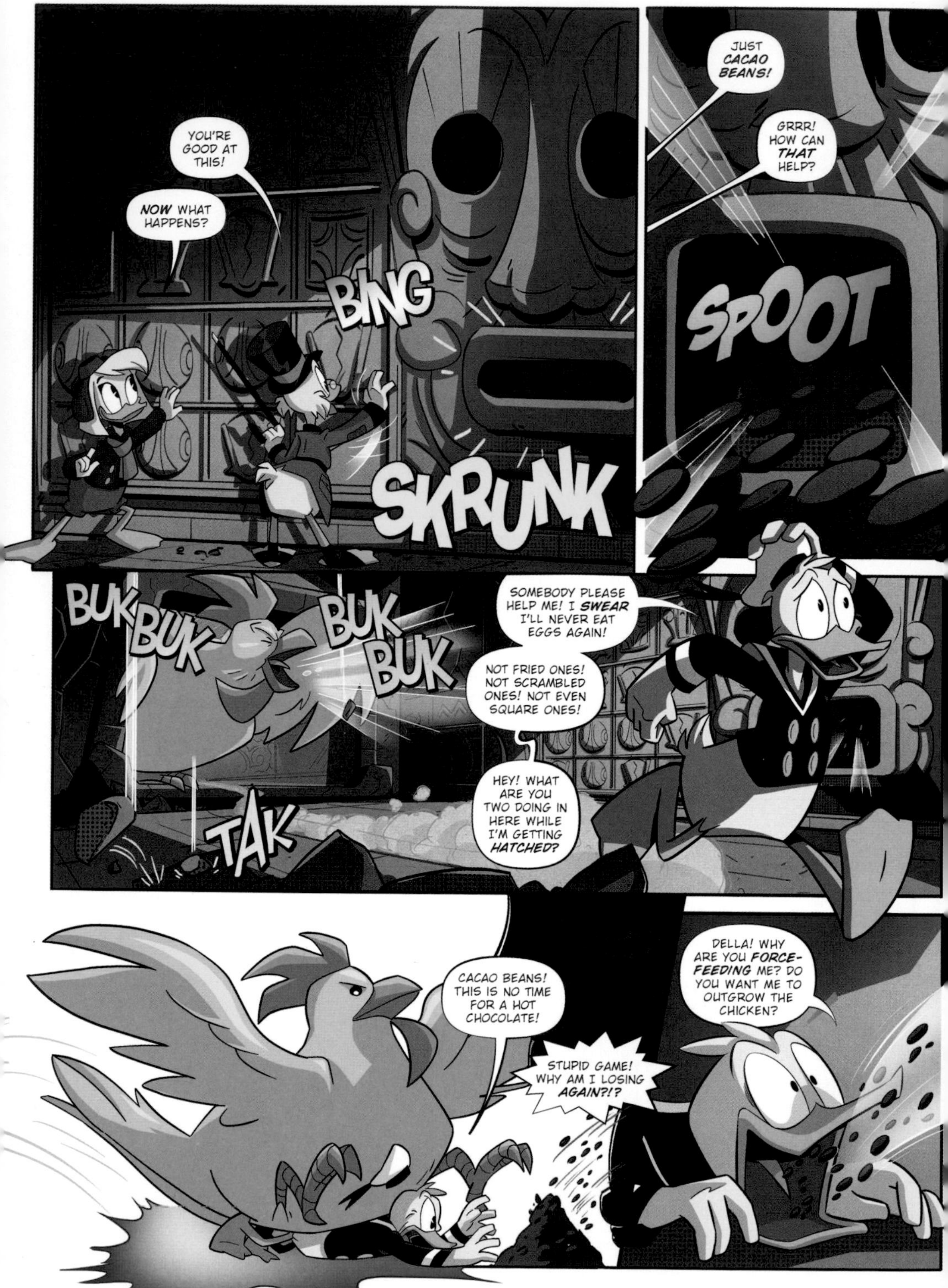
YOU'RE GOOD AT THIS!
NOW WHAT HAPPENS?
BING
SKRUNK
JUST CACAO BEANS!
GRRR! HOW CAN THAT HELP?
SPOOT
BUK BUK
BUK BUK
TAK
SOMEBODY PLEASE HELP ME! I SWEAR I'LL NEVER EAT EGGS AGAIN!
NOT FRIED ONES! NOT SCRAMBLED ONES! NOT EVEN SQUARE ONES!
HEY! WHAT ARE YOU TWO DOING IN HERE WHILE I'M GETTING HATCHED?
CACAO BEANS! THIS IS NO TIME FOR A HOT CHOCOLATE!
STUPID GAME! WHY AM I LOSING AGAIN?!?
DELLA! WHY ARE YOU FORCE-FEEDING ME? DO YOU WANT ME TO OUTGROW THE CHICKEN?

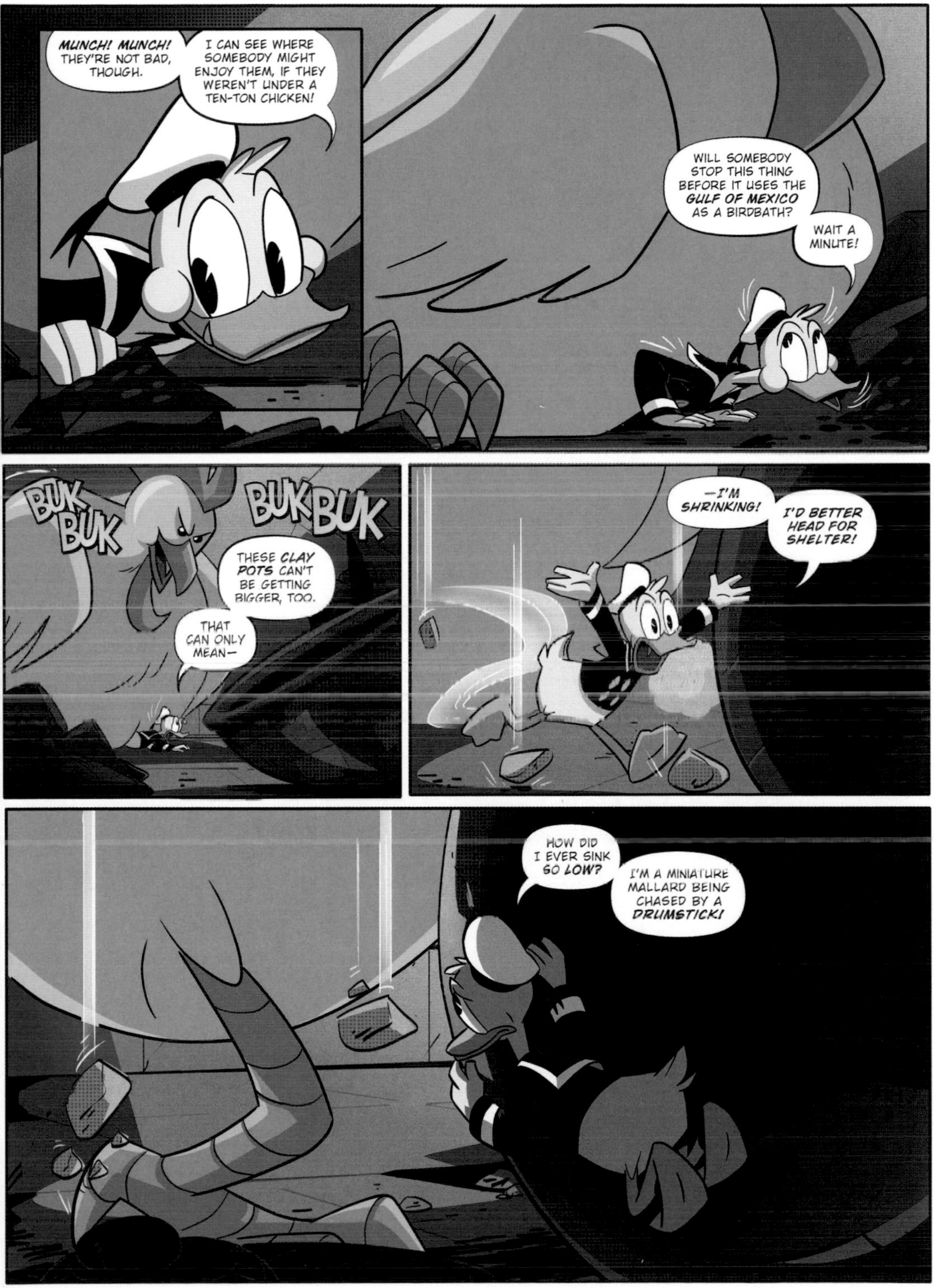
MUNCH! MUNCH! THEY'RE NOT BAD, THOUGH.
I CAN SEE WHERE SOMEBODY MIGHT ENJOY THEM, IF THEY WEREN'T UNDER A TEN-TON CHICKEN!
WILL SOMEBODY STOP THIS THING BEFORE IT USES THE GULF OF MEXICO AS A BIRDBATH?
WAIT A MINUTE!
BUK BUK
BUK BUK
THESE CLAY POTS CAN'T BE GETTING BIGGER, TOO.
THAT CAN ONLY MEAN—
—I'M SHRINKING!
I'D BETTER HEAD FOR SHELTER!
HOW DID I EVER SINK SO LOW?
I'M A MINIATURE MALLARD BEING CHASED BY A DRUMSTICK!

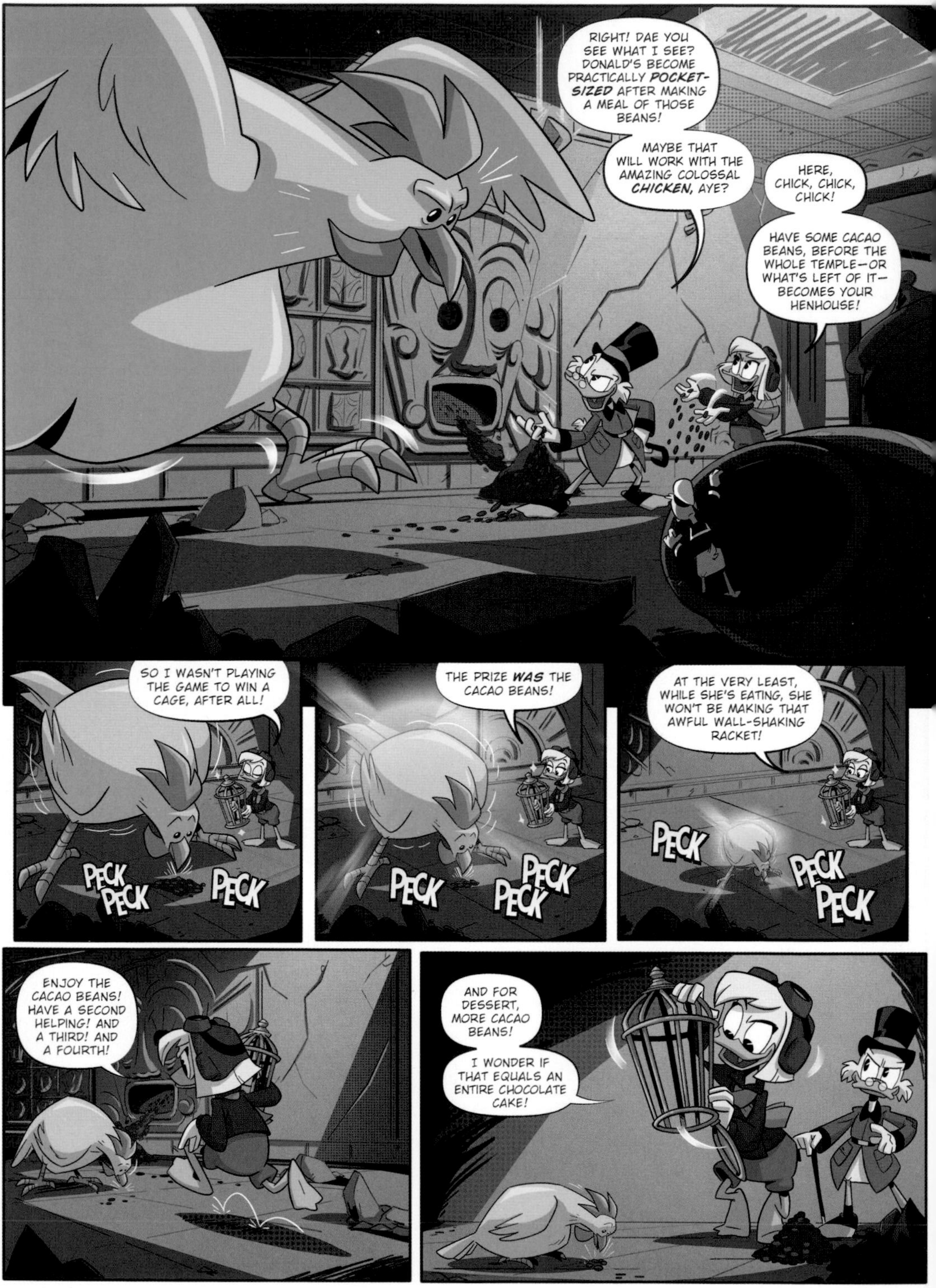
RIGHT! DAE YOU SEE WHAT I SEE? DONALD'S BECOME PRACTICALLY POCKET-SIZED AFTER MAKING A MEAL OF THOSE BEANS!
MAYBE THAT WILL WORK WITH THE AMAZING COLOSSAL CHICKEN, AYE?
HERE, CHICK, CHICK, CHICK!
HAVE SOME CACAO BEANS, BEFORE THE WHOLE TEMPLE—OR WHAT'S LEFT OF IT—BECOMES YOUR HENHOUSE!
SO I WASN'T PLAYING THE GAME TO WIN A CAGE, AFTER ALL!
PECK
PECK
PECK
THE PRIZE WAS THE CACAO BEANS!
PECK
PECK
PECK
AT THE VERY LEAST, WHILE SHE'S EATING, SHE WON'T BE MAKING THAT AWFUL WALL-SHAKING RACKET!
PECK
PECK
PECK
ENJOY THE CACAO BEANS! HAVE A SECOND HELPING! AND A THIRD! AND A FOURTH!
AND FOR DESSERT, MORE CACAO BEANS!
I WONDER IF THAT EQUALS AN ENTIRE CHOCOLATE CAKE!

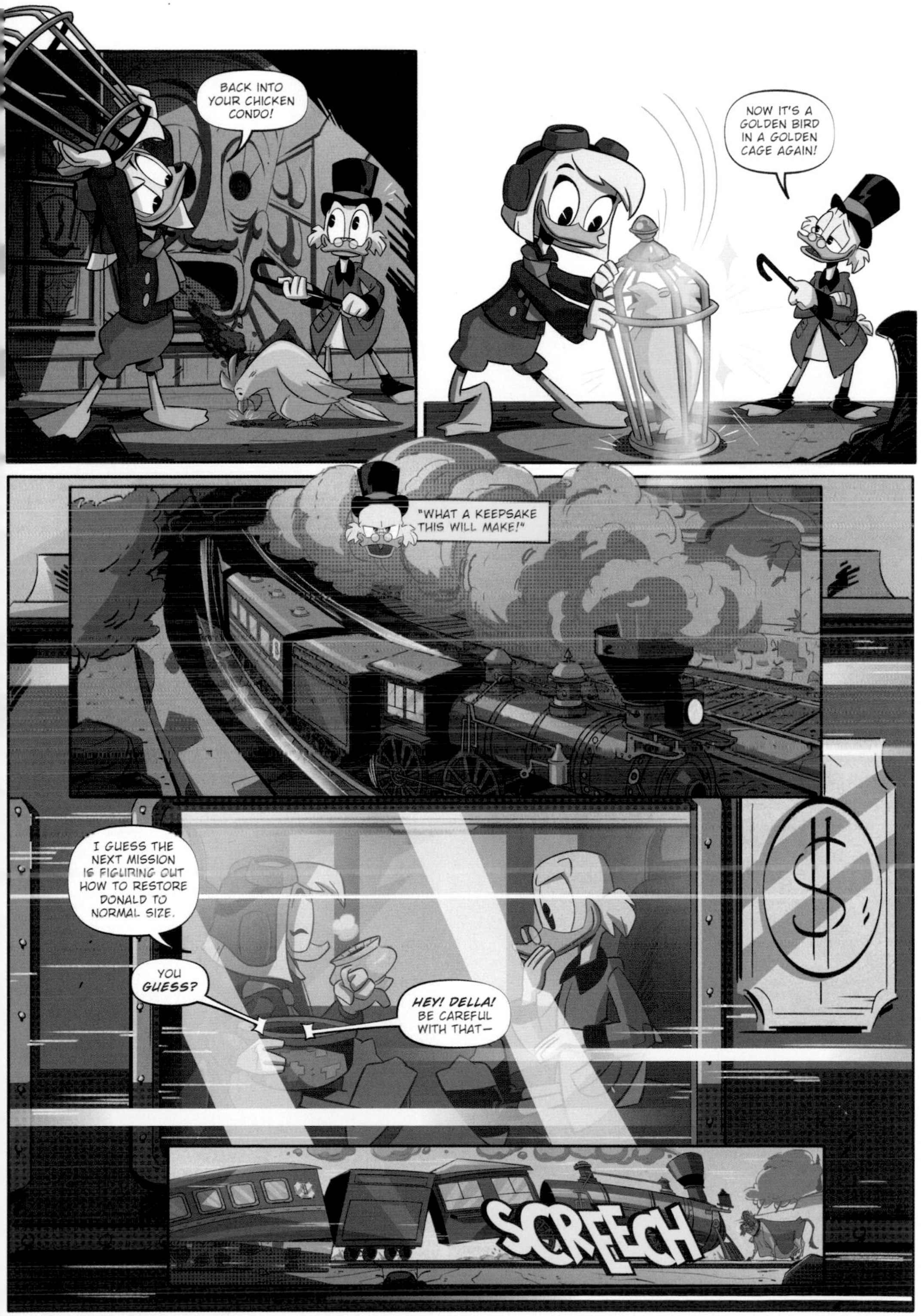
BACK INTO YOUR CHICKEN CONDO!
NOW IT'S A GOLDEN BIRD IN A GOLDEN CAGE AGAIN!
"WHAT A KEEPSAKE THIS WILL MAKE!"
I GUESS THE NEXT MISSION IS FIGURING OUT HOW TO RESTORE DONALD TO NORMAL SIZE.
YOU *GUESS?*
HEY! DELLA! BE CAREFUL WITH THAT—
SCREECH

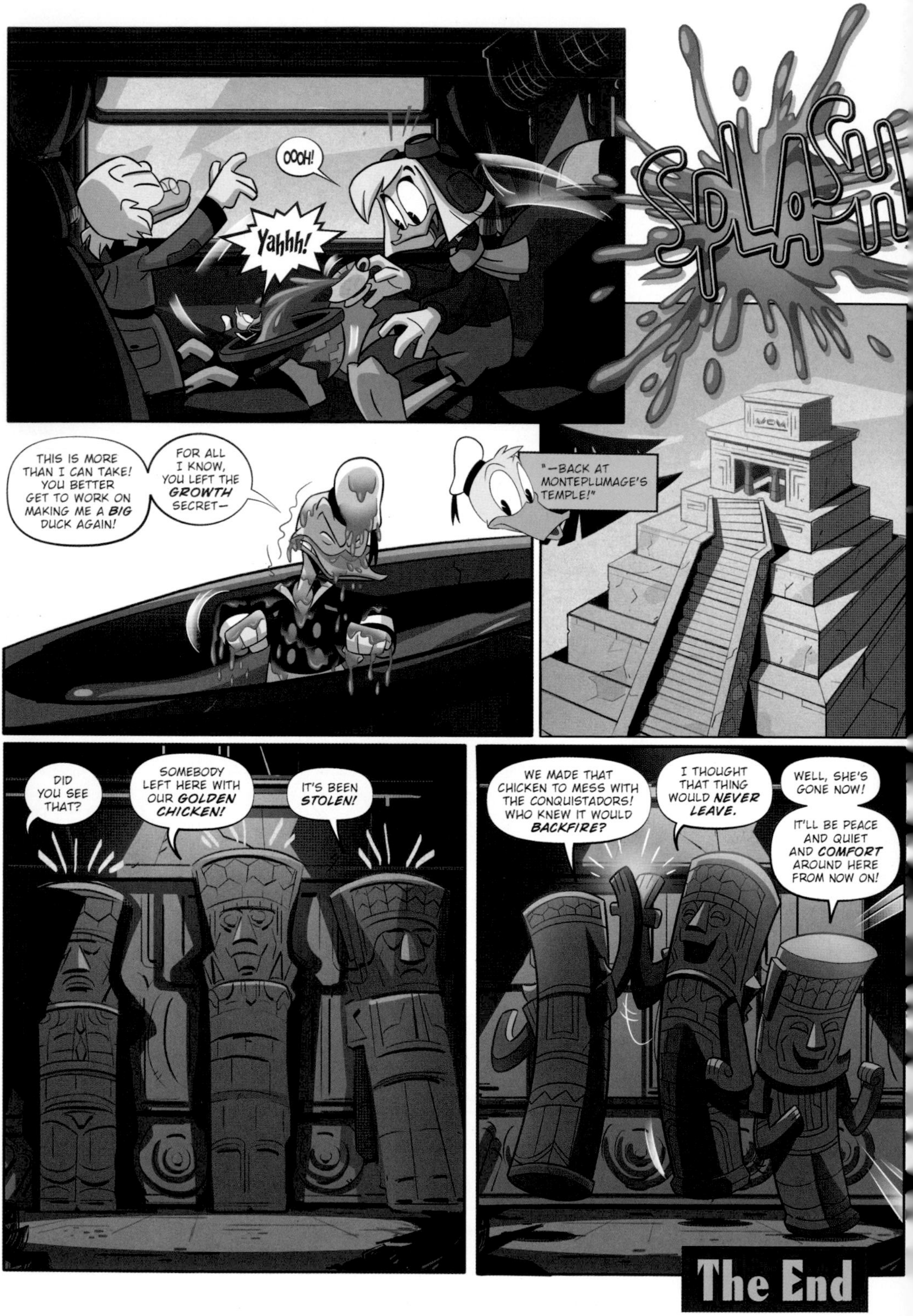
OOOH!
Yahhh!
SPLASH
THIS IS MORE THAN I CAN TAKE! YOU BETTER GET TO WORK ON MAKING ME A BIG DUCK AGAIN!
FOR ALL I KNOW, YOU LEFT THE GROWTH SECRET—
"—BACK AT MONTEPLUMAGE'S TEMPLE!"
DID YOU SEE THAT?
SOMEBODY LEFT HERE WITH OUR GOLDEN CHICKEN!
IT'S BEEN STOLEN!
WE MADE THAT CHICKEN TO MESS WITH THE CONQUISTADORS! WHO KNEW IT WOULD BACKFIRE?
I THOUGHT THAT THING WOULD NEVER LEAVE.
WELL, SHE'S GONE NOW!
IT'LL BE PEACE AND QUIET AND COMFORT AROUND HERE FROM NOW ON!
The End

Disney DuckTales

AWESOME EXPLOITS and QUESTS for rare and wonderful artifacts culled from foreboding terrain and forbidden lands! These are our journeys, these are: The Daring Adventures of Scrooge, Donald and Della Duck!

A VIKING AT MY DOOR!

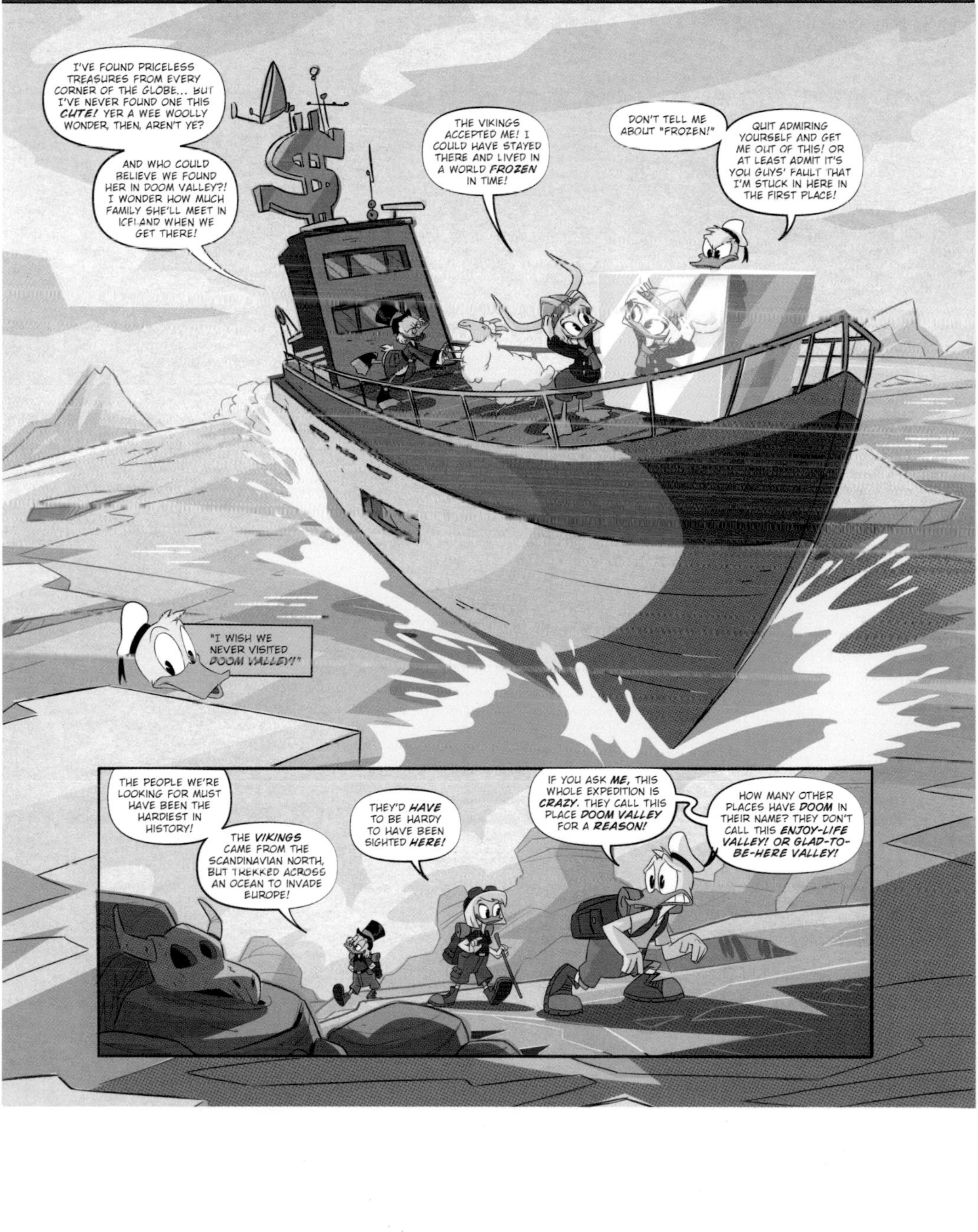

I'VE FOUND PRICELESS TREASURES FROM EVERY CORNER OF THE GLOBE... BUT I'VE NEVER FOUND ONE THIS CUTE! YER A WEE WOOLLY WONDER, THEN, AREN'T YE?
AND WHO COULD BELIEVE WE FOUND HER IN DOOM VALLEY?! I WONDER HOW MUCH FAMILY SHE'LL MEET IN ICELAND WHEN WE GET THERE!
THE VIKINGS ACCEPTED ME! I COULD HAVE STAYED THERE AND LIVED IN A WORLD FROZEN IN TIME!
DON'T TELL ME ABOUT "FROZEN!"
QUIT ADMIRING YOURSELF AND GET ME OUT OF THIS! OR AT LEAST ADMIT IT'S YOU GUYS' FAULT THAT I'M STUCK IN HERE IN THE FIRST PLACE!
"I WISH WE NEVER VISITED DOOM VALLEY!"
THE PEOPLE WE'RE LOOKING FOR MUST HAVE BEEN THE HARDIEST IN HISTORY!
THE VIKINGS CAME FROM THE SCANDINAVIAN NORTH, BUT TREKKED ACROSS AN OCEAN TO INVADE EUROPE!
THEY'D HAVE TO BE HARDY TO HAVE BEEN SIGHTED HERE!
IF YOU ASK ME, THIS WHOLE EXPEDITION IS CRAZY. THEY CALL THIS PLACE DOOM VALLEY FOR A REASON!
HOW MANY OTHER PLACES HAVE DOOM IN THEIR NAME? THEY DON'T CALL THIS ENJOY-LIFE VALLEY! OR GLAD-TO-BE-HERE VALLEY!

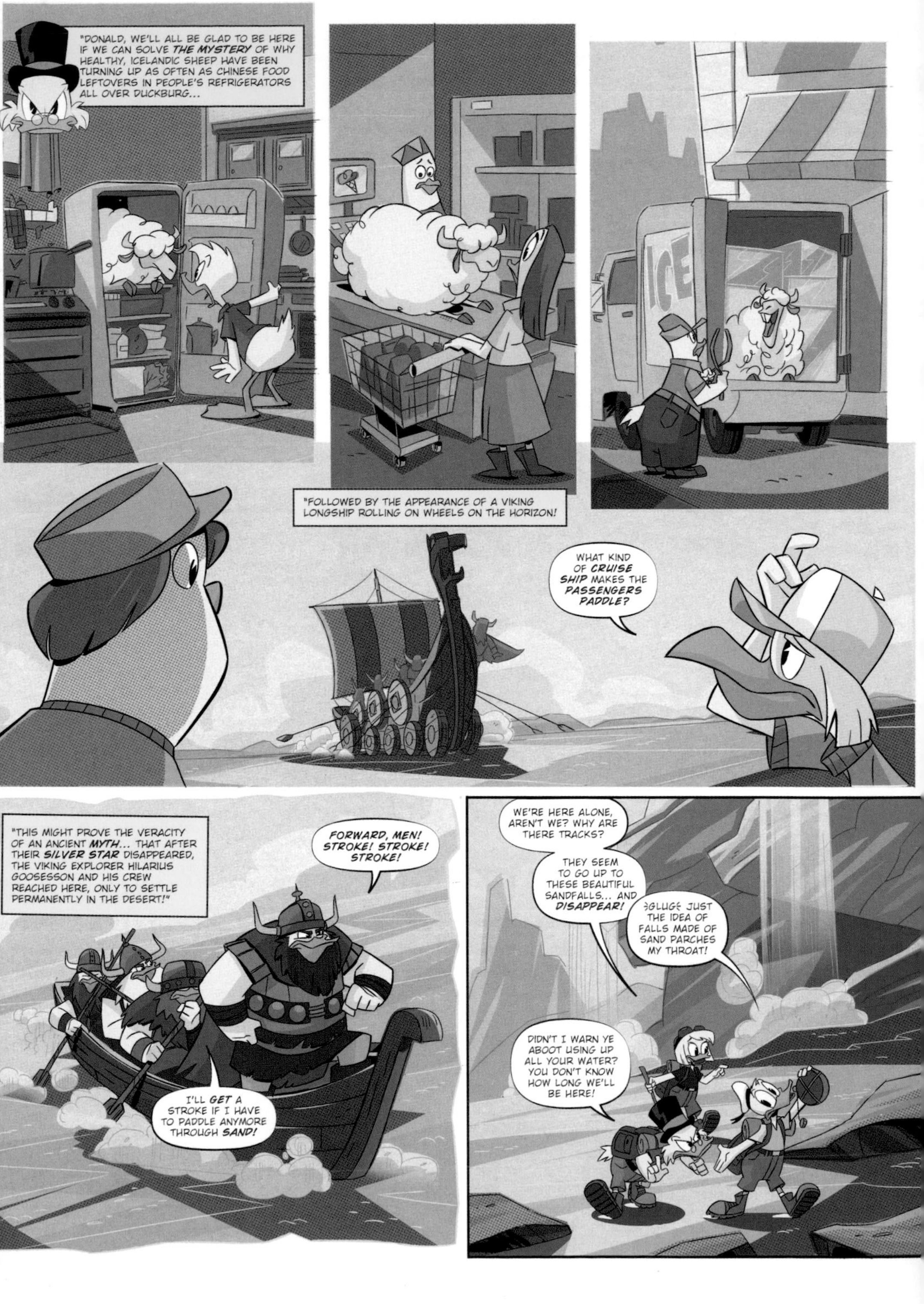
"DONALD, WE'LL ALL BE GLAD TO BE HERE IF WE CAN SOLVE **THE MYSTERY** OF WHY HEALTHY, ICELANDIC SHEEP HAVE BEEN TURNING UP AS OFTEN AS CHINESE FOOD LEFTOVERS IN PEOPLE'S REFRIGERATORS ALL OVER DUCKBURG...
ICE
"FOLLOWED BY THE APPEARANCE OF A VIKING LONGSHIP ROLLING ON WHEELS ON THE HORIZON!
WHAT KIND OF **CRUISE SHIP** MAKES THE **PASSENGERS PADDLE?**
"THIS MIGHT PROVE THE VERACITY OF AN ANCIENT **MYTH**... THAT AFTER THEIR **SILVER STAR** DISAPPEARED, THE VIKING EXPLORER HILARIUS GOOSESSON AND HIS CREW REACHED HERE, ONLY TO SETTLE PERMANENTLY IN THE DESERT!"
FORWARD, MEN! STROKE! STROKE! STROKE!
I'LL **GET** A STROKE IF I HAVE TO PADDLE ANYMORE THROUGH **SAND!**
WE'RE HERE ALONE, AREN'T WE? WHY ARE THERE TRACKS?
THEY SEEM TO GO UP TO THESE BEAUTIFUL SANDFALLS... AND **DISAPPEAR!**
GLUG JUST THE IDEA OF FALLS MADE OF SAND PARCHES MY THROAT!
DIDN'T I WARN YE ABOOT USING UP ALL YOUR WATER? YOU DON'T KNOW HOW LONG WE'LL BE HERE!

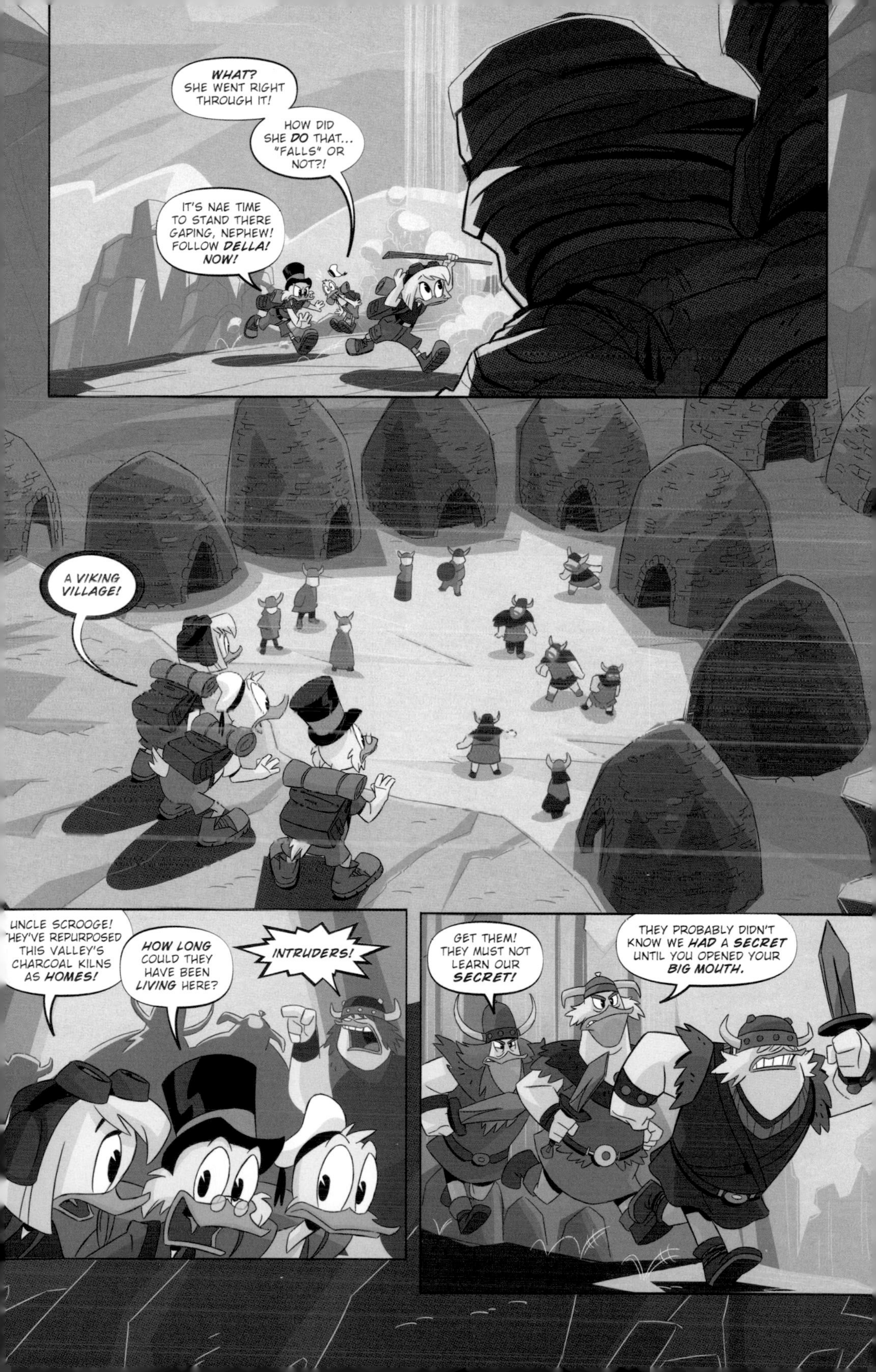
WHAT? SHE WENT RIGHT THROUGH IT!
HOW DID SHE DO THAT... "FALLS" OR NOT?!
IT'S NAE TIME TO STAND THERE GAPING, NEPHEW! FOLLOW DELLA! NOW!
A VIKING VILLAGE!
UNCLE SCROOGE! THEY'VE REPURPOSED THIS VALLEY'S CHARCOAL KILNS AS HOMES!
HOW LONG COULD THEY HAVE BEEN LIVING HERE?
INTRUDERS!
GET THEM! THEY MUST NOT LEARN OUR SECRET!
THEY PROBABLY DIDN'T KNOW WE HAD A SECRET UNTIL YOU OPENED YOUR BIG MOUTH.

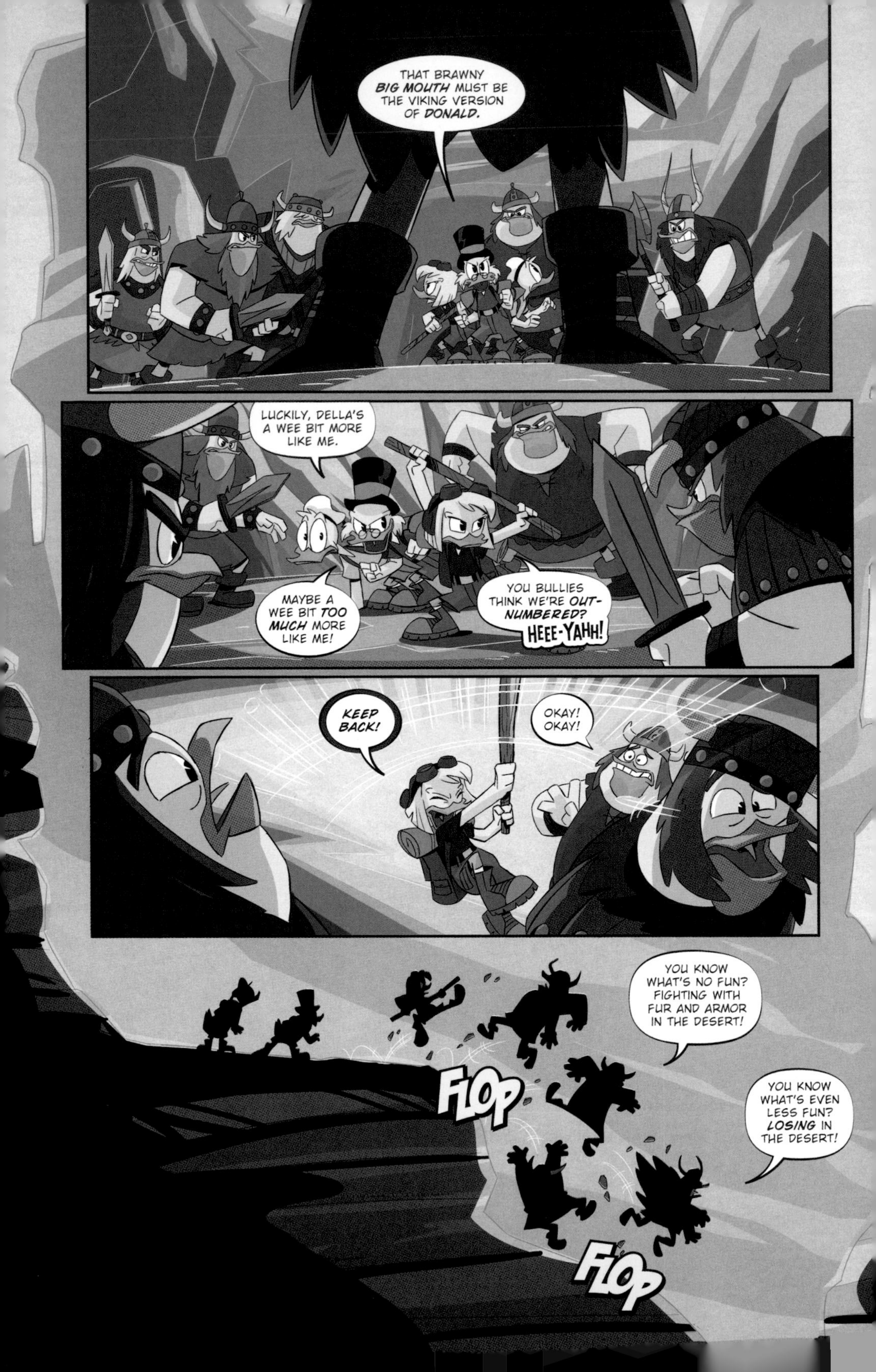
THAT BRAWNY BIG MOUTH MUST BE THE VIKING VERSION OF DONALD.
LUCKILY, DELLA'S A WEE BIT MORE LIKE ME.
MAYBE A WEE BIT TOO MUCH MORE LIKE ME!
YOU BULLIES THINK WE'RE OUT-NUMBERED? HEEE-YAHH!
KEEP BACK!
OKAY! OKAY!
YOU KNOW WHAT'S NO FUN? FIGHTING WITH FUR AND ARMOR IN THE DESERT!
YOU KNOW WHAT'S EVEN LESS FUN? LOSING IN THE DESERT!
FLOP
FLOP

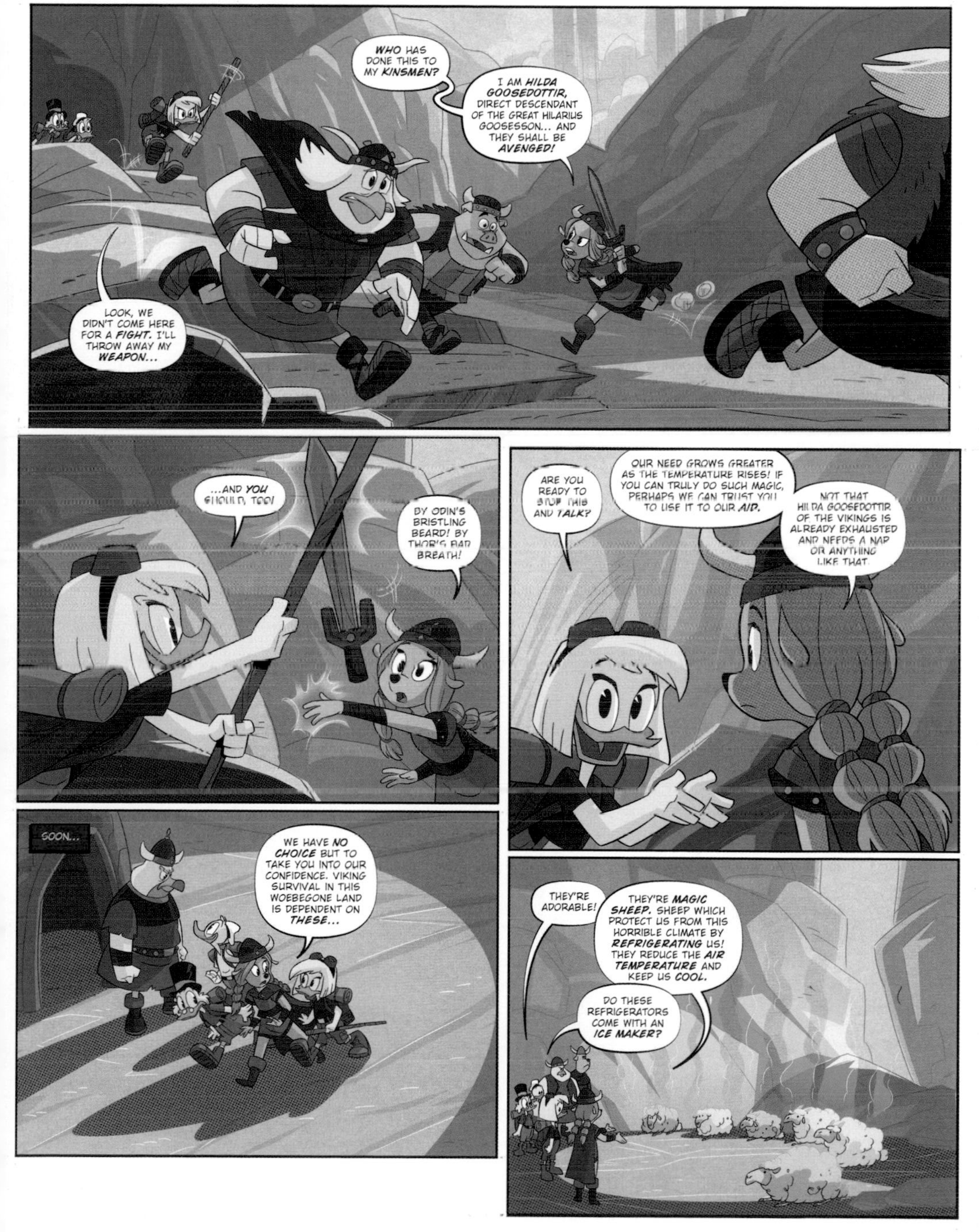
WHO HAS DONE THIS TO MY KINSMEN?
I AM HILDA GOOSEDOTTIR, DIRECT DESCENDANT OF THE GREAT HILARIUS GOOSESSON... AND THEY SHALL BE AVENGED!
LOOK, WE DIDN'T COME HERE FOR A FIGHT. I'LL THROW AWAY MY WEAPON...
...AND YOU SHOULD, TOO!
BY ODIN'S BRISTLING BEARD! BY THOR'S BAD BREATH!
ARE YOU READY TO STOP THIS AND TALK?
OUR NEED GROWS GREATER AS THE TEMPERATURE RISES! IF YOU CAN TRULY DO SUCH MAGIC, PERHAPS WE CAN TRUST YOU TO USE IT TO OUR AID.
NOT THAT HILDA GOOSEDOTTIR OF THE VIKINGS IS ALREADY EXHAUSTED AND NEEDS A NAP OR ANYTHING LIKE THAT.
SOON...
WE HAVE NO CHOICE BUT TO TAKE YOU INTO OUR CONFIDENCE. VIKING SURVIVAL IN THIS WOEBEGONE LAND IS DEPENDENT ON THESE...
THEY'RE ADORABLE!
THEY'RE MAGIC SHEEP. SHEEP WHICH PROTECT US FROM THIS HORRIBLE CLIMATE BY REFRIGERATING US! THEY REDUCE THE AIR TEMPERATURE AND KEEP US COOL.
DO THESE REFRIGERATORS COME WITH AN ICE MAKER?

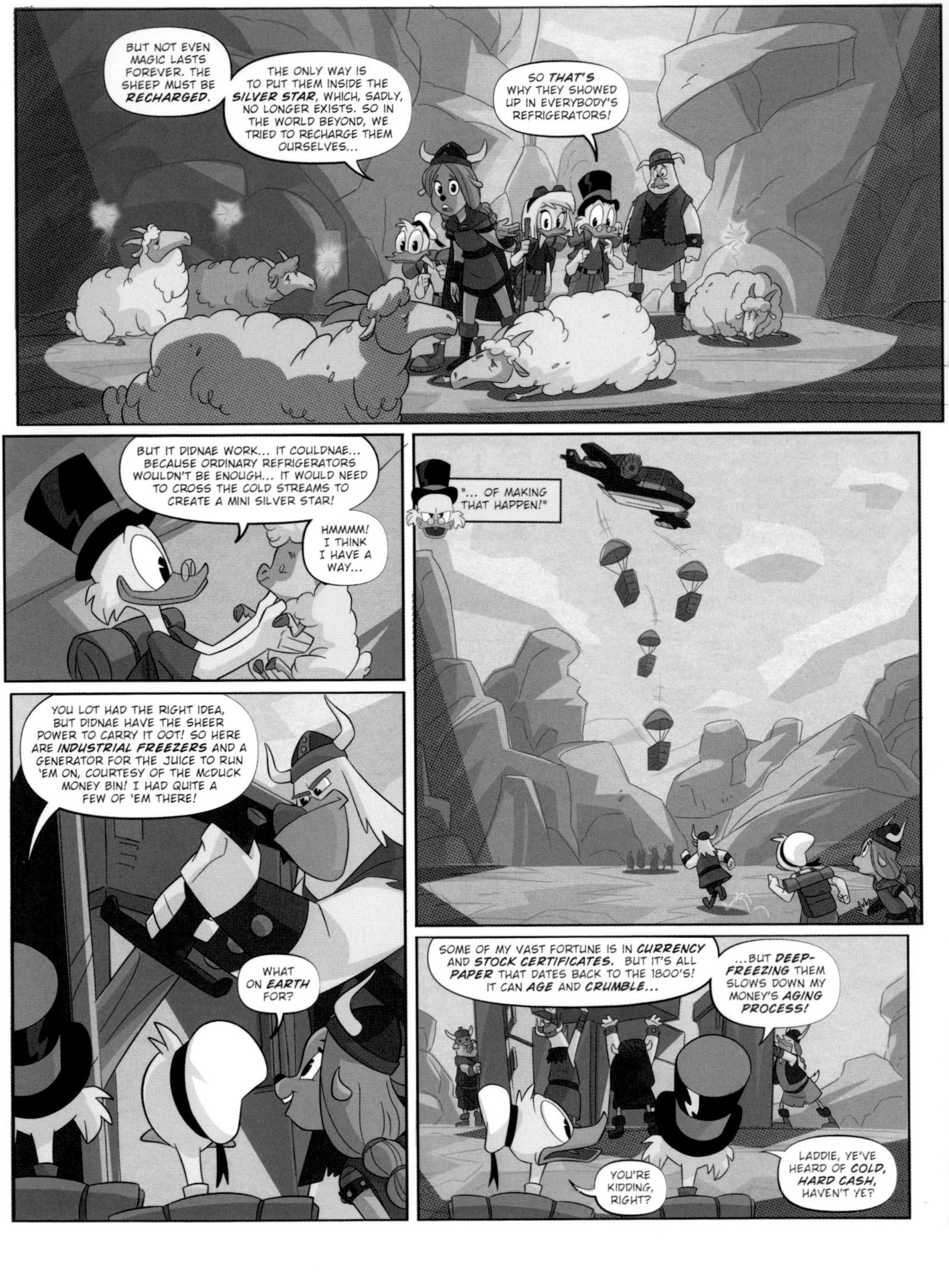
BUT NOT EVEN MAGIC LASTS FOREVER. THE SHEEP MUST BE RECHARGED.
THE ONLY WAY IS TO PUT THEM INSIDE THE SILVER STAR, WHICH, SADLY, NO LONGER EXISTS. SO IN THE WORLD BEYOND, WE TRIED TO RECHARGE THEM OURSELVES...
SO THAT'S WHY THEY SHOWED UP IN EVERYBODY'S REFRIGERATORS!
BUT IT DIDNAE WORK... IT COULDNAE... BECAUSE ORDINARY REFRIGERATORS WOULDN'T BE ENOUGH... IT WOULD NEED TO CROSS THE COLD STREAMS TO CREATE A MINI SILVER STAR!
HMMMM! I THINK I HAVE A WAY...
"... OF MAKING THAT HAPPEN!"
YOU LOT HAD THE RIGHT IDEA, BUT DIDNAE HAVE THE SHEER POWER TO CARRY IT OOT! SO HERE ARE INDUSTRIAL FREEZERS AND A GENERATOR FOR THE JUICE TO RUN 'EM ON, COURTESY OF THE McDUCK MONEY BIN! I HAD QUITE A FEW OF 'EM THERE!
WHAT ON EARTH FOR?
SOME OF MY VAST FORTUNE IS IN CURRENCY AND STOCK CERTIFICATES. BUT IT'S ALL PAPER THAT DATES BACK TO THE 1800'S! IT CAN AGE AND CRUMBLE...
...BUT DEEP-FREEZING THEM SLOWS DOWN MY MONEY'S AGING PROCESS!
YOU'RE KIDDING, RIGHT?
LADDIE, YE'VE HEARD OF COLD, HARD CASH, HAVEN'T YE?

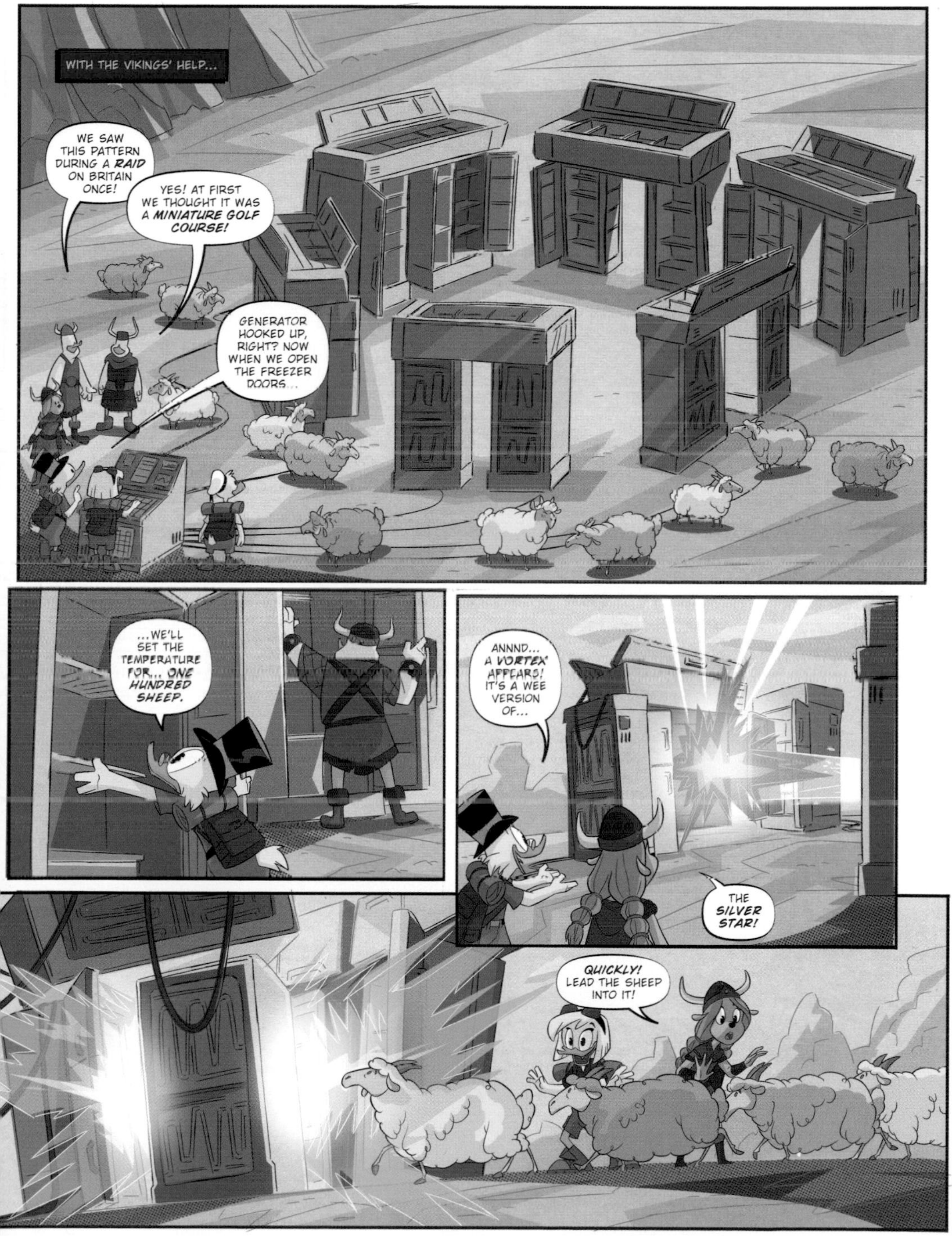

WITH THE VIKINGS' HELP...
WE SAW THIS PATTERN DURING A RAID ON BRITAIN ONCE!
YES! AT FIRST WE THOUGHT IT WAS A MINIATURE GOLF COURSE!
GENERATOR HOOKED UP, RIGHT? NOW WHEN WE OPEN THE FREEZER DOORS...
...WE'LL SET THE TEMPERATURE FOR... ONE HUNDRED SHEEP.
ANNND... A VORTEX APPEARS! IT'S A WEE VERSION OF...
THE SILVER STAR!
QUICKLY! LEAD THE SHEEP INTO IT!

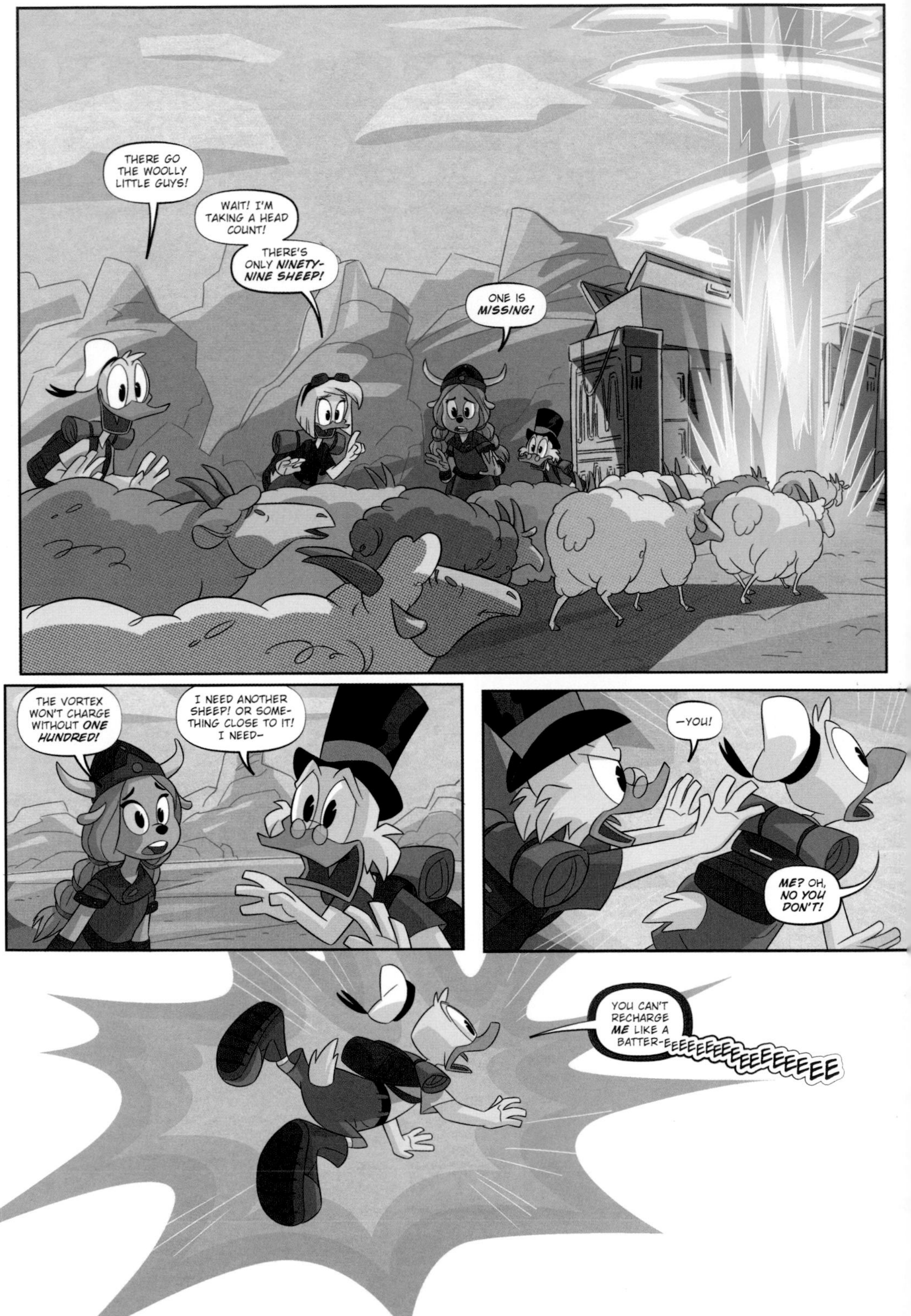
THERE GO THE WOOLLY LITTLE GUYS!
WAIT! I'M TAKING A HEAD COUNT!
THERE'S ONLY NINETY-NINE SHEEP!
ONE IS MISSING!
THE VORTEX WON'T CHARGE WITHOUT ONE HUNDRED!
I NEED ANOTHER SHEEP! OR SOMETHING CLOSE TO IT! I NEED–
–YOU!
ME? OH, NO YOU DON'T!
YOU CAN'T RECHARGE ME LIKE A BATTER-EEEEEEEEEEEEEEEEE

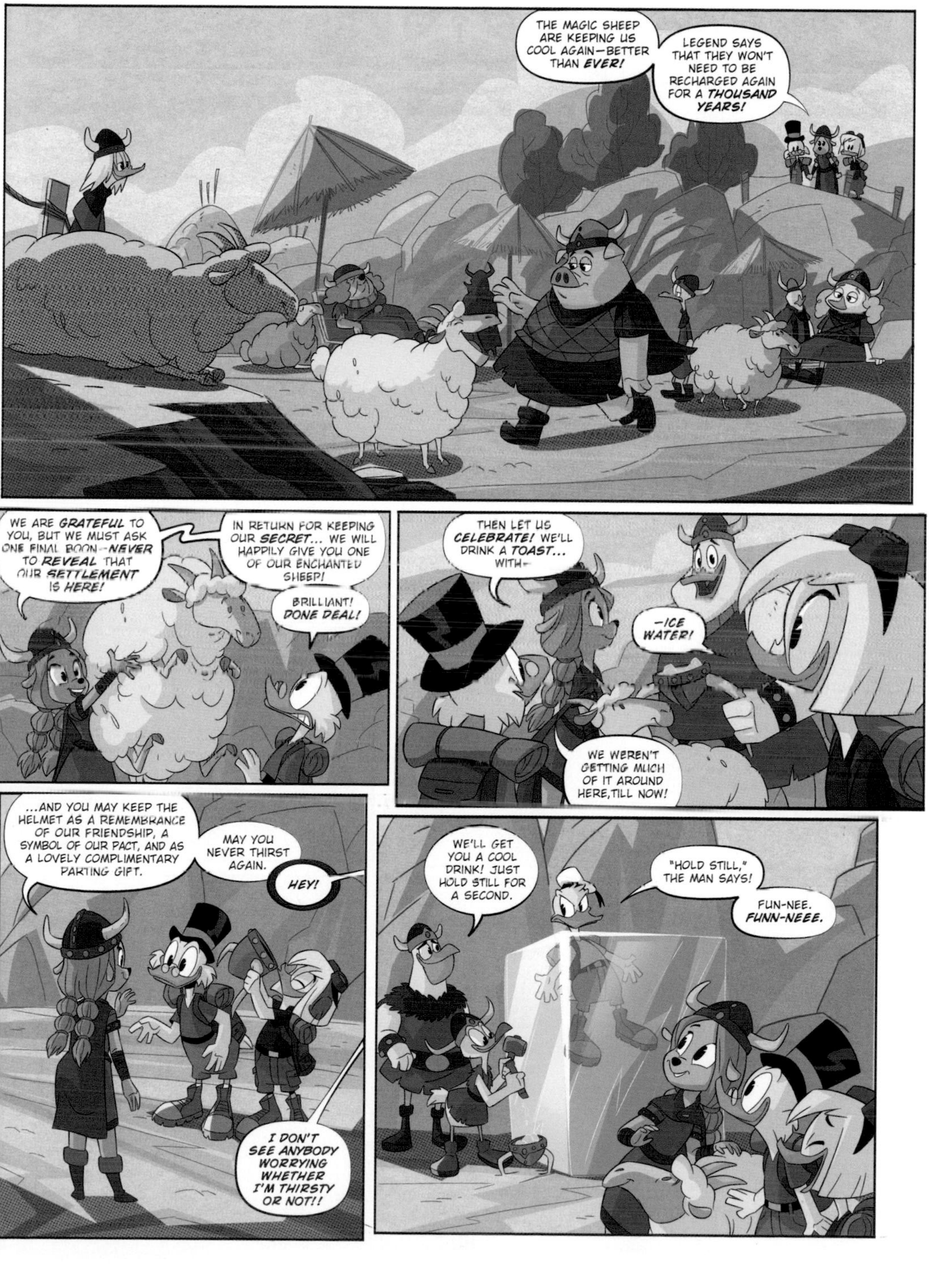
THE MAGIC SHEEP ARE KEEPING US COOL AGAIN—BETTER THAN EVER!
LEGEND SAYS THAT THEY WON'T NEED TO BE RECHARGED AGAIN FOR A THOUSAND YEARS!
WE ARE GRATEFUL TO YOU, BUT WE MUST ASK ONE FINAL BOON--NEVER TO REVEAL THAT OUR SETTLEMENT IS HERE!
IN RETURN FOR KEEPING OUR SECRET... WE WILL HAPPILY GIVE YOU ONE OF OUR ENCHANTED SHEEP!
BRILLIANT! DONE DEAL!
THEN LET US CELEBRATE! WE'LL DRINK A TOAST... WITH—
—ICE WATER!
WE WEREN'T GETTING MUCH OF IT AROUND HERE,TILL NOW!
...AND YOU MAY KEEP THE HELMET AS A REMEMBRANCE OF OUR FRIENDSHIP, A SYMBOL OF OUR PACT, AND AS A LOVELY COMPLIMENTARY PARTING GIFT.
MAY YOU NEVER THIRST AGAIN.
HEY!
I DON'T SEE ANYBODY WORRYING WHETHER I'M THIRSTY OR NOT!!
WE'LL GET YOU A COOL DRINK! JUST HOLD STILL FOR A SECOND.
"HOLD STILL," THE MAN SAYS!
FUN-NEE. FUNN-NEEE.

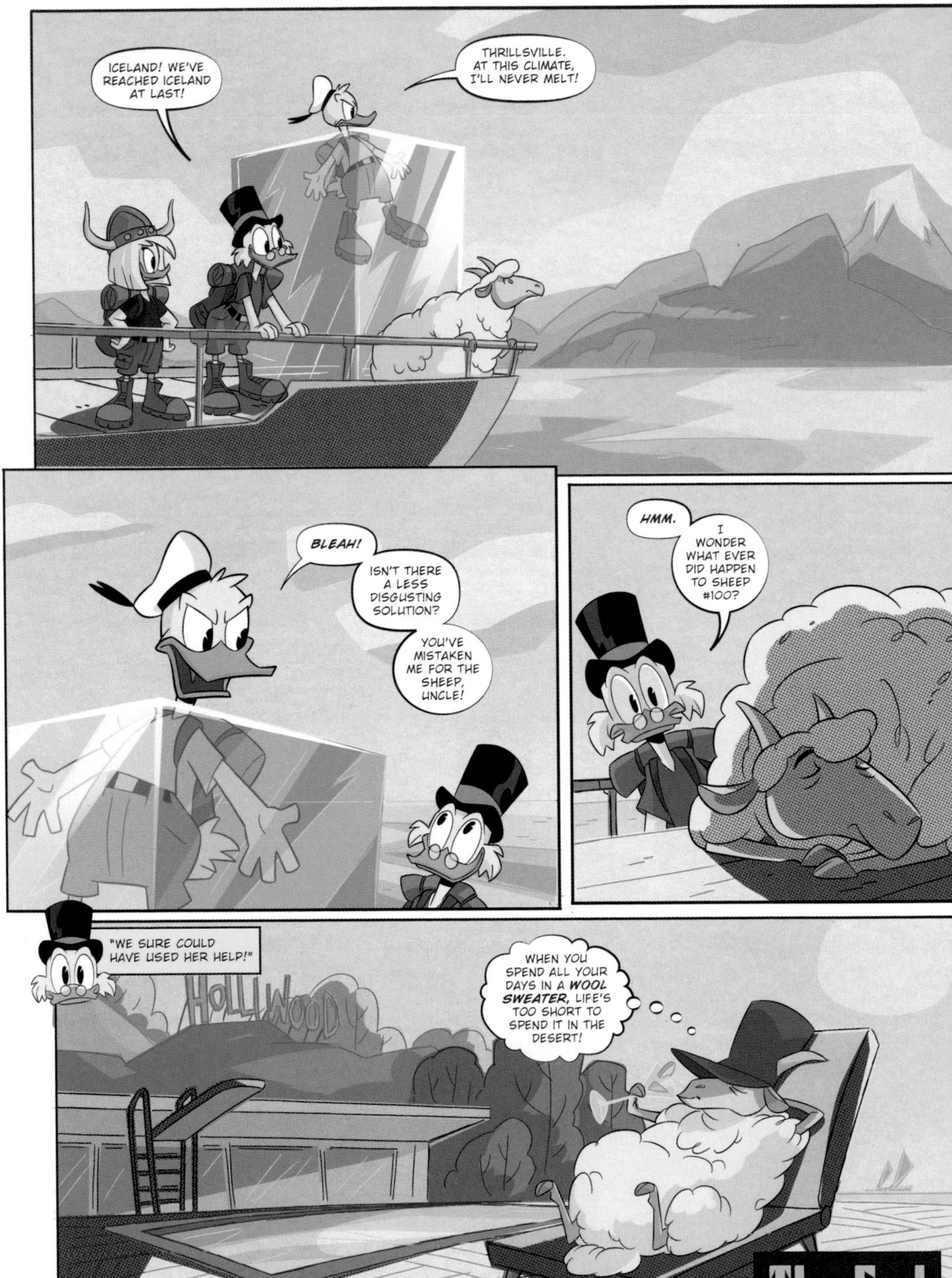
ICELAND! WE'VE REACHED ICELAND AT LAST!
THRILLSVILLE. AT THIS CLIMATE, I'LL NEVER MELT!
BLEAH!
ISN'T THERE A LESS DISGUSTING SOLUTION?
YOU'VE MISTAKEN ME FOR THE SHEEP, UNCLE!
HMM.
I WONDER WHAT EVER DID HAPPEN TO SHEEP #100?
"WE SURE COULD HAVE USED HER HELP!"
HOLLYWOOD
WHEN YOU SPEND ALL YOUR DAYS IN A WOOL SWEATER, LIFE'S TOO SHORT TO SPEND IT IN THE DESERT!
The End

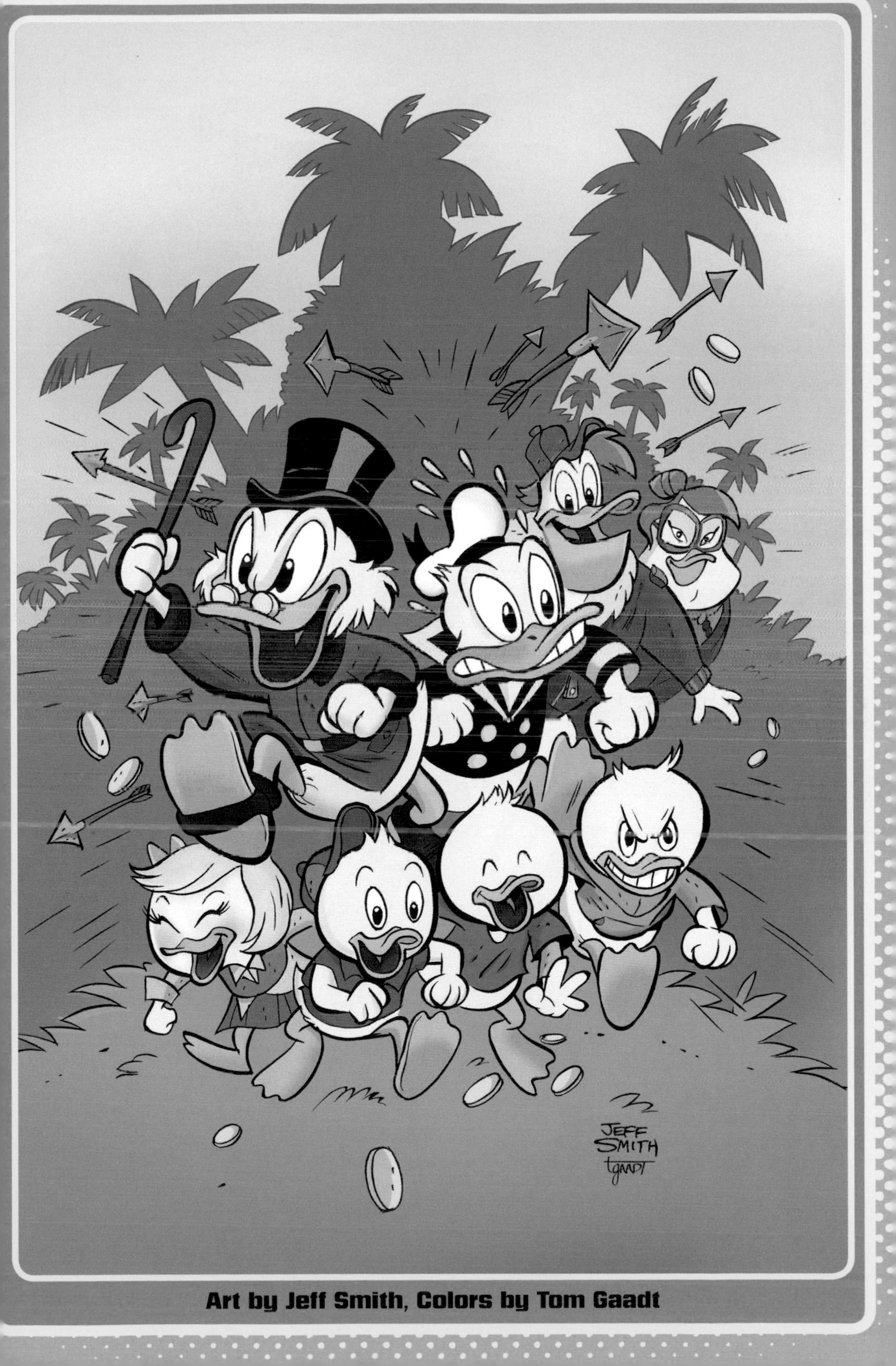
JEFF SMITH
tgaadt

Art by Jeff Smith, Colors by Tom Gaadt

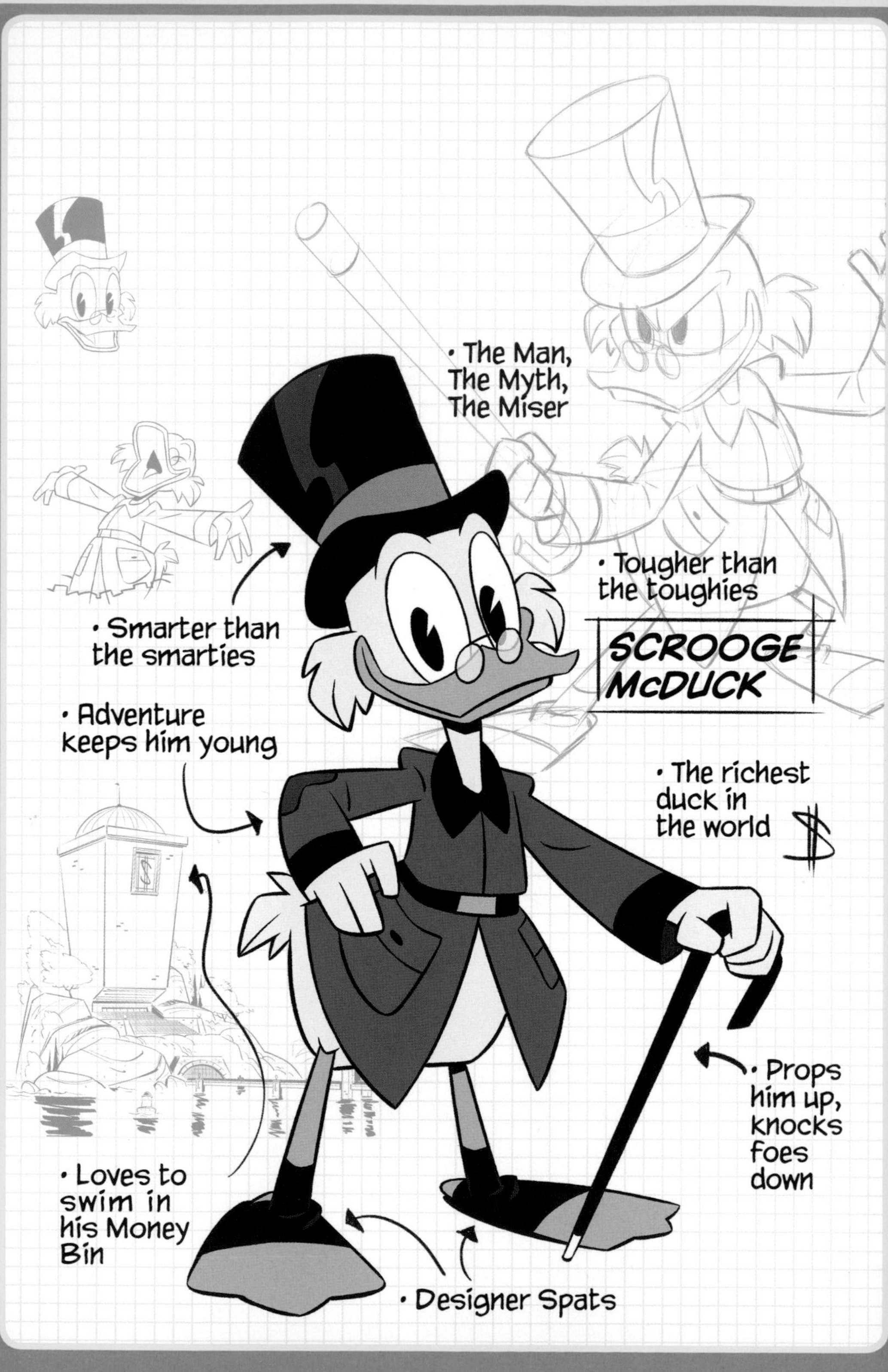

• The Man, The Myth, The Miser
• Tougher than the toughies
SCROOGE McDUCK
• Smarter than the smarties
• Adventure keeps him young
• The richest duck in the world
• Props him up, knocks foes down
• Loves to swim in his Money Bin
• Designer Spats

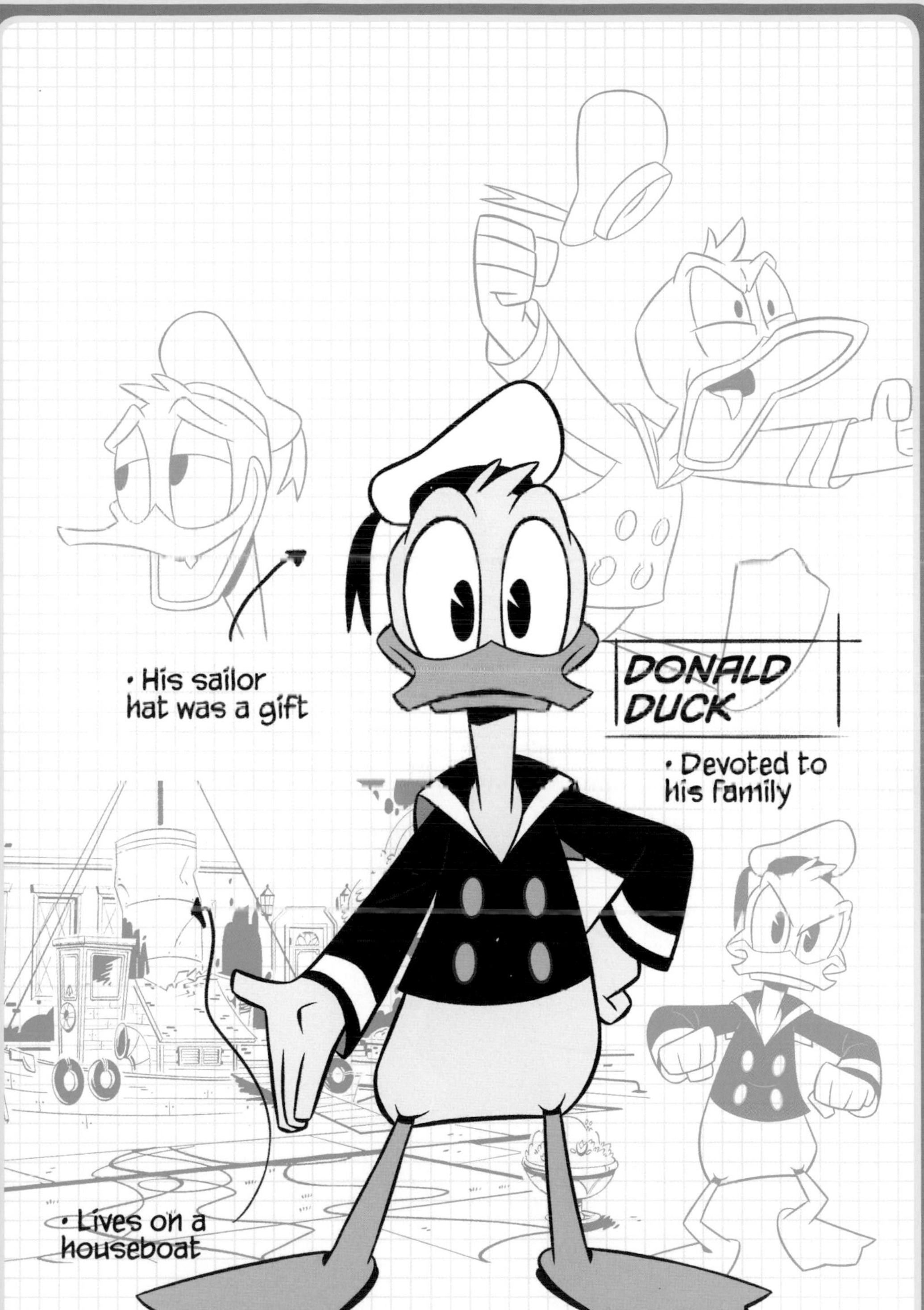

DONALD DUCK
• His sailor hat was a gift
• Devoted to his family
• Lives on a houseboat

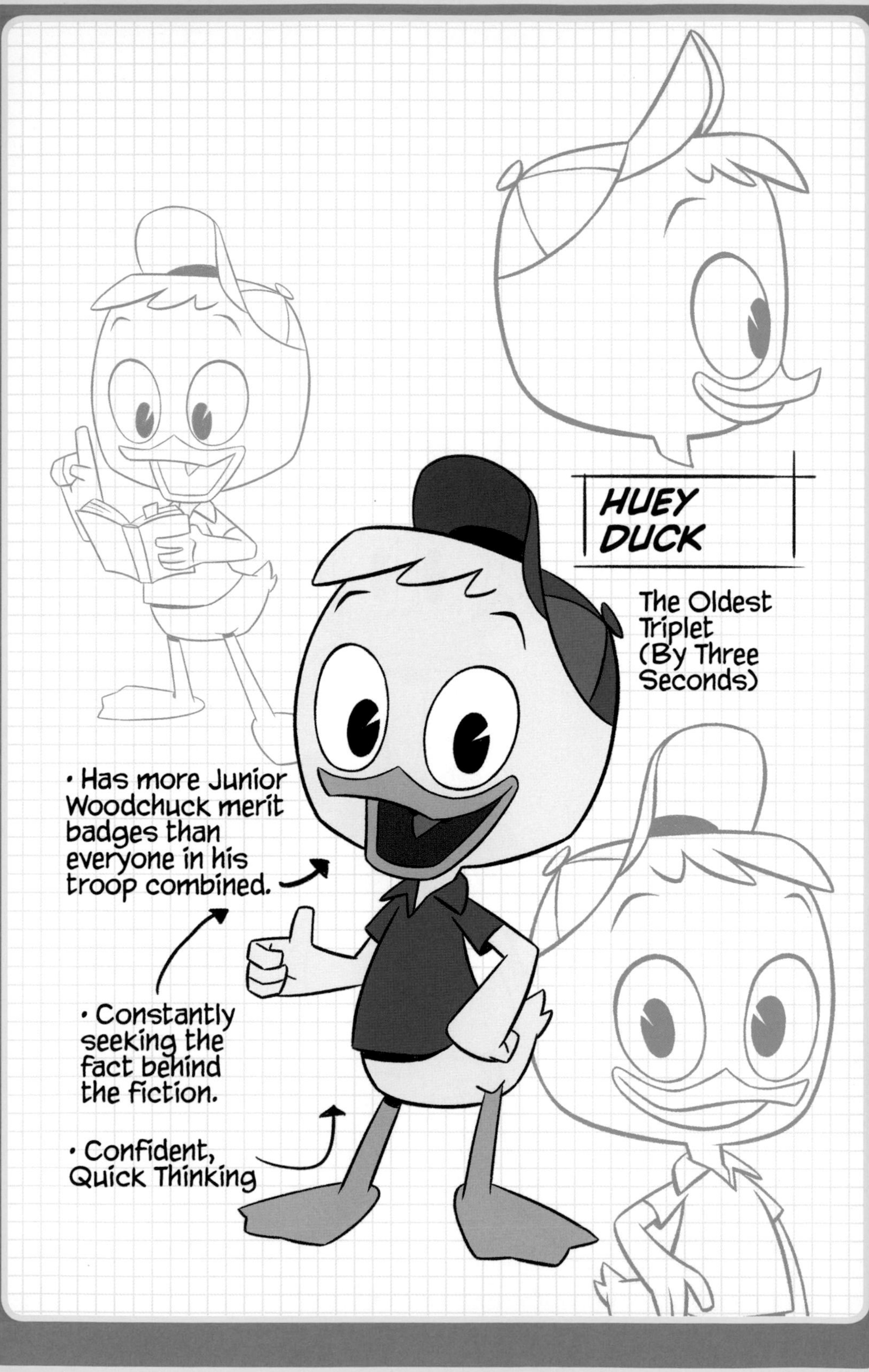
HUEY DUCK
The Oldest Triplet (By Three Seconds)
• Has more Junior Woodchuck merit badges than everyone in his troop combined.
• Constantly seeking the fact behind the fiction.
• Confident, Quick Thinking

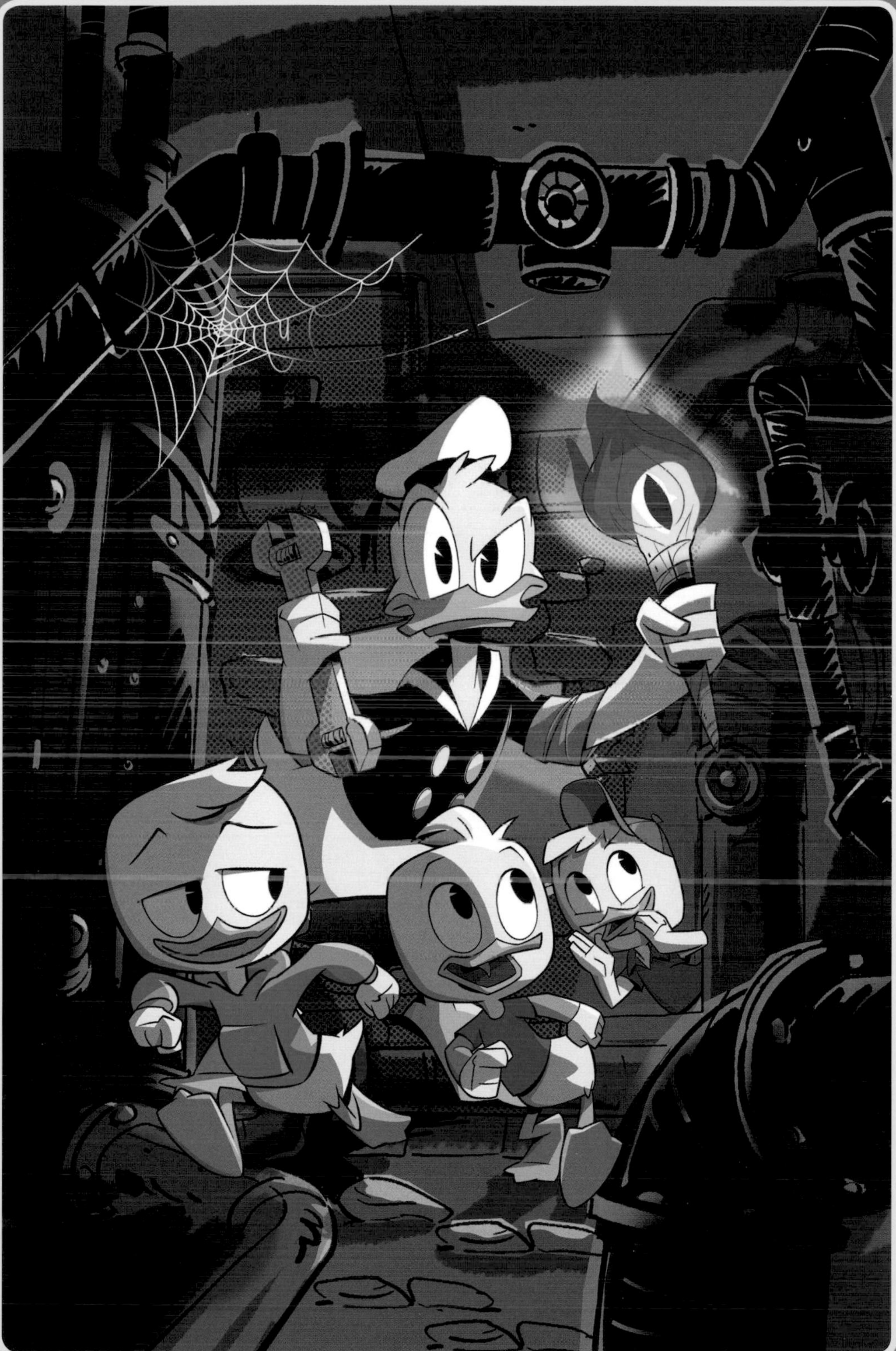

Art by Marco Ghiglione, Colors by Lucio De Guiseppe

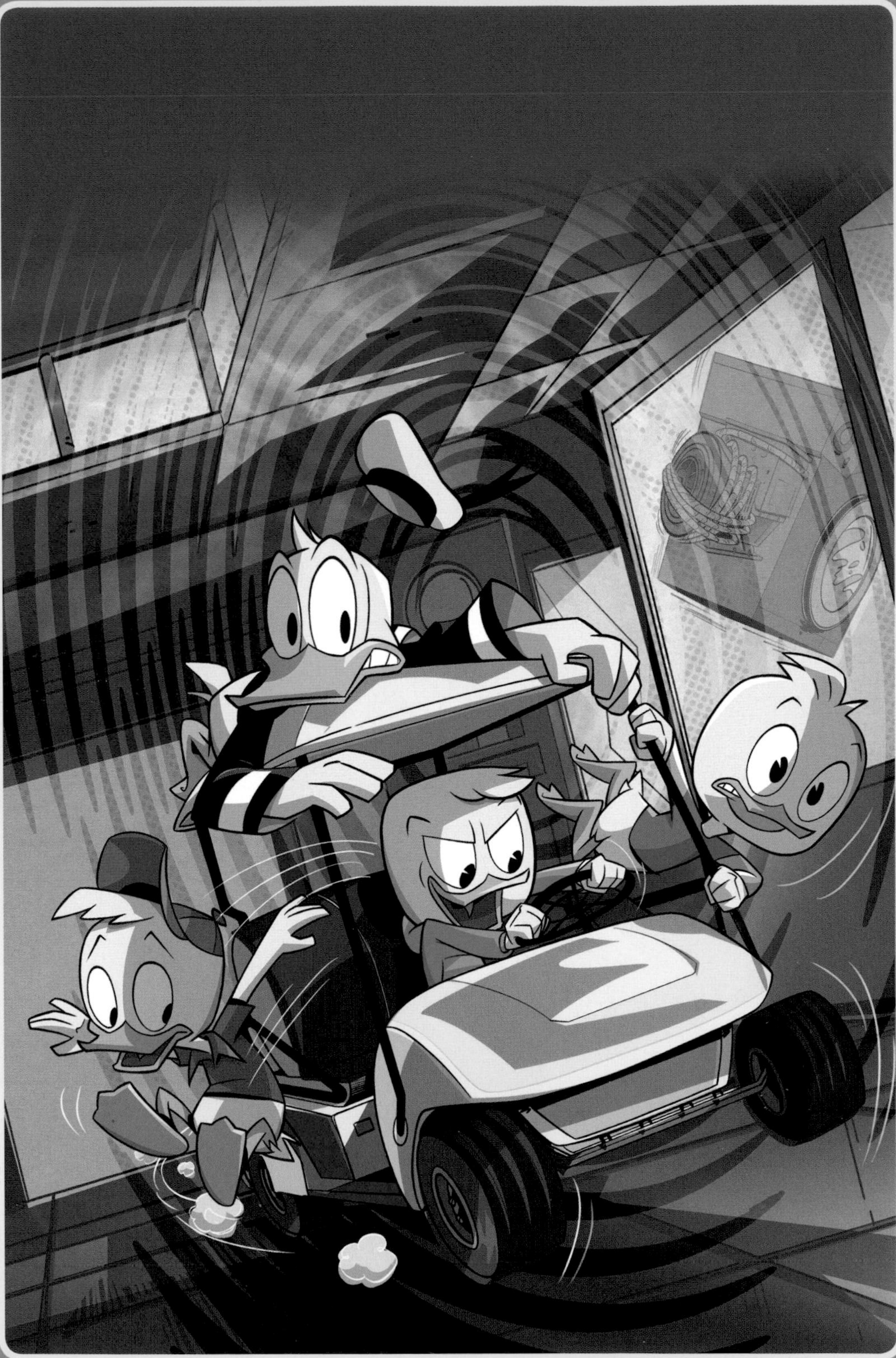

Art by Marco Ghiglione, Colors by Lucio De Guiseppe

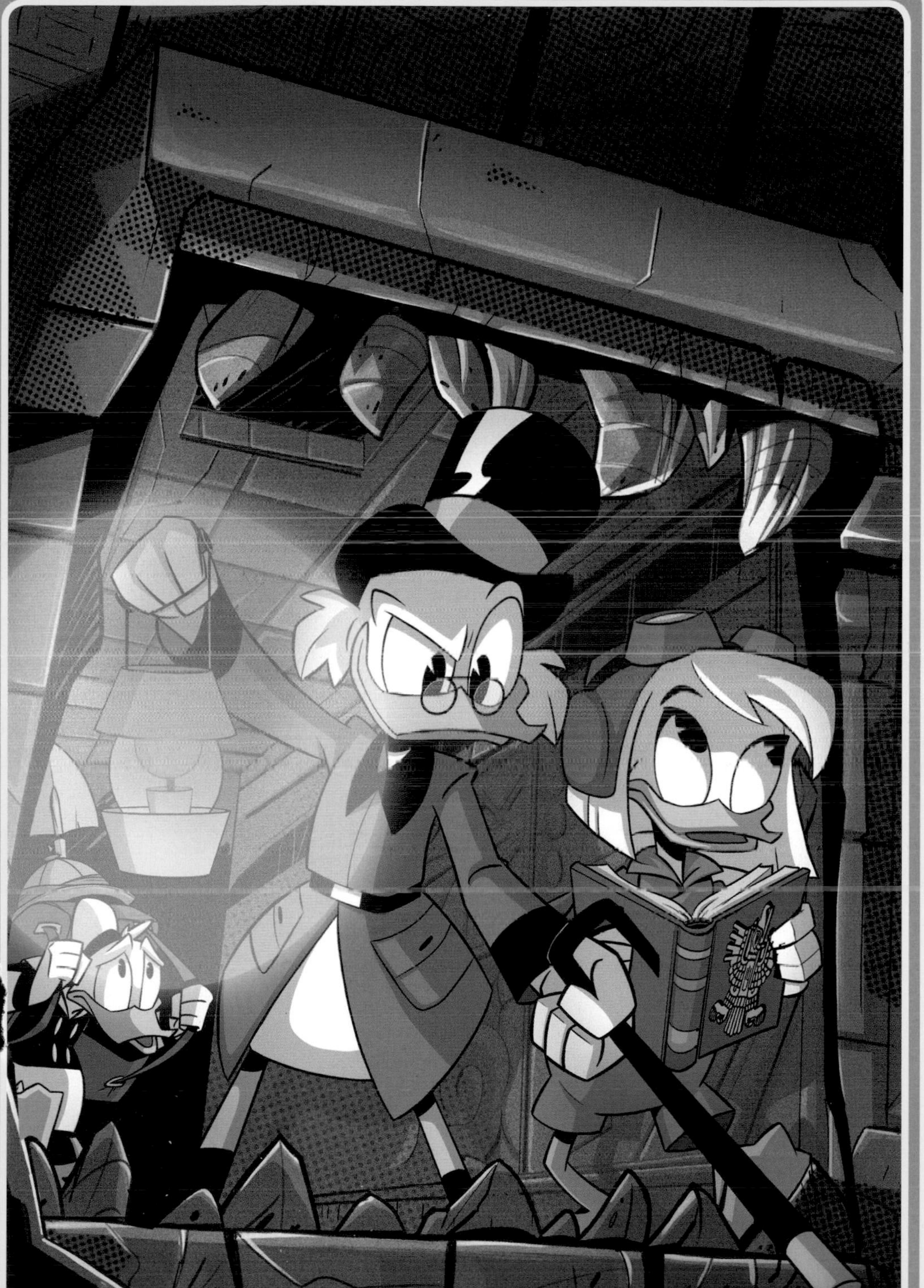

Art by Marco Ghiglione, Colors by Kawaii Studio

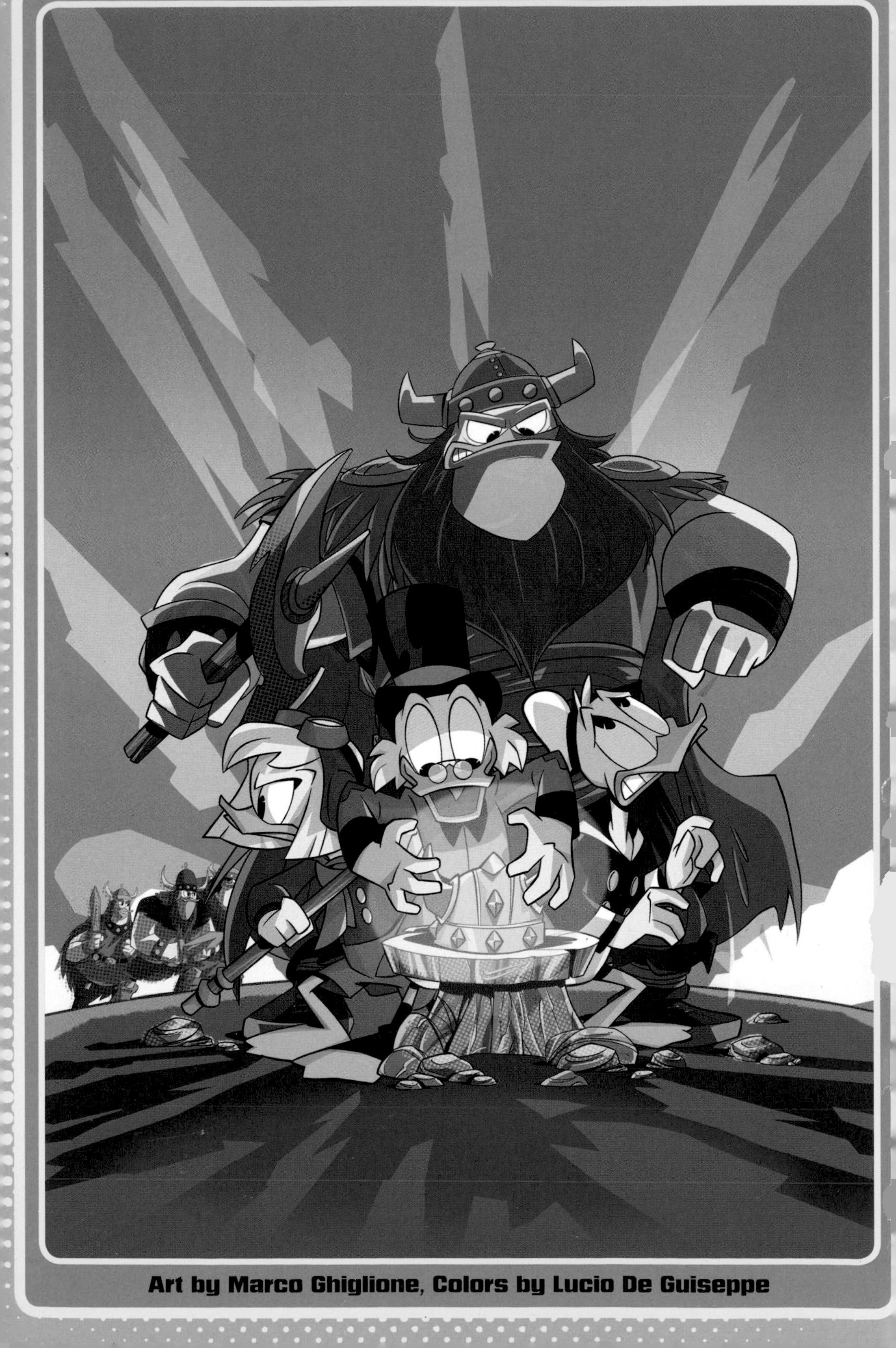

Art by Marco Ghiglione, Colors by Lucio De Guiseppe